BYE-BYE, BIRDIE

Staying well away from the Ovaro's tracks, Fargo returned to the oak. He jumped, caught hold of the low limb, and pulled himself up. Moving to a higher branch, he sat and put the Henry across his legs. Off through the trees the rider appeared.

A white man in a high-crowned hat and a cowhide vest and a flannel shirt and chaps. In a holster high on the man's right hip was a Starr revolver. Fargo raised the Henry to his shoulder.

The man appeared to be in his thirties, maybe early forties. He had a square, rugged face sprinkled with stubble. He was broad across the chest and sat the saddle like someone born to it. His gaze was on the ground.

Fargo let the rider get almost to the oak and then he levered a round into the chamber and said, "Tweet, tweet."

The man jerked his head up and drew rein and started to draw but froze when he saw the Henry pointed at him . . .

THE
TRAILSMAN
#342

ROCKY
MOUNTAIN
REVENGE

by

Jon Sharpe

A SIGNET BOOK

SIGNET
Published by New American Library, a division of
Penguin Group (USA) Inc., 375 Hudson Street,
New York, New York 10014, USA
Penguin Group (Canada), 90 Eglinton Avenue East, Suite 700, Toronto,
Ontario M4P 2Y3, Canada (a division of Pearson Penguin Canada Inc.)
Penguin Books Ltd., 80 Strand, London WC2R 0RL, England
Penguin Ireland, 25 St. Stephen's Green, Dublin 2,
Ireland (a division of Penguin Books Ltd.)
Penguin Group (Australia), 250 Camberwell Road, Camberwell, Victoria 3124,
Australia (a division of Pearson Australia Group Pty. Ltd.)
Penguin Books India Pvt. Ltd., 11 Community Centre, Panchsheel Park,
New Delhi - 110 017, India
Penguin Group (NZ), 67 Apollo Drive, Rosedale, North Shore 0632,
New Zealand (a division of Pearson New Zealand Ltd.)
Penguin Books (South Africa) (Pty.) Ltd., 24 Sturdee Avenue,
Rosebank, Johannesburg 2196, South Africa

Penguin Books Ltd., Registered Offices:
80 Strand, London WC2R 0RL, England

First published by Signet, an imprint of New American Library,
a division of Penguin Group (USA) Inc.

First Printing, April 2010
10 9 8 7 6 5 4 3 2 1

The first chapter of this book previously appeared in *Sierra Six-Guns*, the three hundred
forty-first volume in this series.

Copyright © Penguin Group (USA) Inc., 2010
All rights reserved

 REGISTERED TRADEMARK—MARCA REGISTRADA

Printed in the United States of America

The Trailsman

Beginnings . . . they bend the tree and they mark the man. Skye Fargo was born when he was eighteen. Terror was his midwife, vengeance his first cry. Killing spawned Skye Fargo, ruthless, cold-blooded murder. Out of the acrid smoke of gunpowder still hanging in the air, he rose, cried out a promise never forgotten.

The Trailsman they began to call him all across the West: searcher, scout, hunter, the man who could see where others only looked, his skills for hire but not his soul, the man who lived each day to the fullest, yet trailed each tomorrow. Skye Fargo, the Trailsman, the seeker who could take the wildness of a land and the wanting of a woman and make them his own.

The Rockies, 1860—where the stakes are higher than the mountain peaks, and death crouches in the shadows beside every trail.

1

Someone was stalking Skye Fargo.

As usual, Fargo was up at the pink tinge of dawn. The mornings were chill that deep in the Green River country, and the first thing he did was rekindle the fire and put what was left of last night's coffee on. He sat cross-legged, letting the flames warm him, and gazed at the pink to the east.

Fargo's lake blue eyes narrowed. For an instant he thought he saw the silhouette of a rider in the distance. He blinked, and it was gone. He watched for it to reappear and when it didn't he held his hands to the crackling flames and listened to his stomach growl.

Fargo opened his saddlebags. He took out a bundle of pemmican wrapped in rabbit fur, unwrapped the fur, and bit into a piece.

This was the life Fargo liked best, just him and the Ovaro, wandering where the wind took them. For a while, anyway. His poke was almost empty and soon he must give thought to filling it. Not that he cared all that much about money. If he did, he wouldn't make his living as a scout and tracker and whatever else chance tossed his way.

When the Arbuckle's was hot, Fargo poured a steaming cup full. He held the cup in both hands and sipped and felt it warm him down to his toes. He looked to the east and saw the silhouette again. The rider was coming over the crest of a hill and dipped into dense timber.

Fargo's brow puckered. The rider was coming from the

same direction he had. In fact, the rider appeared to be smack on his trail. It could be coincidence but Fargo hadn't survived as long as he had by assuming people always had the best of intentions.

He finished the cup and poured another. He usually had two, sometimes more. Coffee cost money and he hated to waste it. By the time he was done the sun was up and the world around him was rosy and warm. He doused the fire and rolled up his blankets. He threw his saddle blanket on the Ovaro and then the saddle. He collected his saddlebags, tied his bedroll, and was ready to ride out.

Fargo checked to the east. The rider wasn't in sight. He forked leather, the saddle creaking under him, lifted the reins, and lightly touched his spurs to the stallion. He rode to the northwest. He was in no particular hurry.

The forest was alive with wildlife. Robins and sparrows and jays warbled and chirped and squawked. A raven flapped overhead. A startled rabbit bounded away. A pair of does raised their tails and fled in high leaps. A cow elk crashed through the brush, snorting in annoyance at being disturbed.

Fargo climbed to the top of a hill and drew rein. Shifting in the saddle, he stared down at the meadow. In a while the rider emerged from the trees and went to the exact spot where Fargo had camped. The man dismounted and knelt and put his hands to the embers.

"I'll be damned." So far as Fargo was aware, he didn't have any enemies out to kill him. Not at the moment, anyway. He'd made more than a few. It came from his knack for running into folks who thought they had the god-given right to ride roughshod over everyone else. He couldn't abide that. Step on his toes and there was hell to pay.

Fargo reined around and rode on. He wasn't overly worried. Whoever was after him was a good tracker but he was in his element. Few knew the wilds as well as he did. Few knew as many tricks to stay alive.

He went about a mile, enough to give the man hunting him

the idea that he didn't suspect anything. Then he cast about for a likely spot. An oak tree with a low limb caught his eye. He rode directly under it and went another hundred yards before he drew rein. Swinging down, he tied the Ovaro behind a spruce and shucked his Henry from the saddle scabbard.

Staying well away from the Ovaro's tracks, he returned to the oak. He jumped, caught hold of the low limb, and pulled himself up. Moving to a higher branch, he sat with his back to the bole and put the Henry across his legs.

"Come and get me, you son of a bitch."

The minutes crawled. A squirrel scampered among the treetops. He was glad it didn't notice him. The racket it would make would alert the rider.

A golden finch and its mate landed on a nearby limb and flew off in alarm when they saw him.

A hoof thudded dully.

Fargo fixed his gaze on the Ovaro's tracks. Off through the trees the rider appeared. A white man in a high-crowned hat and a cowhide vest and a flannel shirt and chaps. In a holster high on the man's right hip was a Starr revolver.

Fargo raised the Henry to his shoulder.

The man appeared to be in his thirties, maybe early forties. He had a square, rugged face sprinkled with stubble. He was broad across the chest and sat the saddle like someone born to it. His gaze was on the ground.

Fargo let the rider get almost to the oak and then he levered a round into the chamber and said, "Tweet, tweet."

The man jerked his head up and drew rein and started to draw but froze when he saw the Henry pointed at him.

"Take your hand off the six-gun."

The man did.

"Raise your arms and keep them where I can see them."

The man did.

"Now give me a good reason why I shouldn't blow out your wick."

"You'd kill a man for nothing?" The rider's voice was deep and low, almost as deep and low as Fargo's.

"Do I look green behind the ears?" Fargo rejoined. "I don't like being hunted. So think fast and make it good." He noticed that the man wasn't tense or anxious or upset. Most would be, with a rifle held on them.

"I have been hunting you, yes."

"You admit it?"

"Why wouldn't I? I don't have anything to hide. I'm not out to do you in, if that's what you're thinking. If I was, you wouldn't have caught on to me."

"Brag a lot, do you?"

The man grinned. "My handle is Stoddard. Jim Stoddard. I work for Clarence Bell of the Circle B. Could be you've heard of him."

"Could be I haven't."

"The Circle B is up to the Sweetwater River country. In ten years it will be the biggest ranch in these or any other parts."

"You ride for the brand?"

"That I do. I'm a puncher. But I hunted a lot as a kid and I'm a fair hand at tracking so Mr. Bell sent me to find you."

"How in hell did you know I was even in the territory?"

"Mr. Bell had a letter to send east. We went to Sweetwater Station the day after you shot that gent who cheated you at cards."

Fargo sighed. The Central, Overland, California, and Pikes Peak Express Company ran a stage line from Saint Louis to Salt Lake City. Sweetwater Station was a stage stop. There was also a saloon. He'd stopped for a drink and a friendly game of cards but the game didn't stay friendly and he had to shoot a two-bit gambler who had a card rig up his sleeve.

"The barkeep told Mr. Bell and mentioned as you were almost as famous as Kit Carson and Jim Bridger."

"Oh, hell."

"Mr. Bell sent me after you and here I am," Stoddard concluded his account. "Now if you'll climb down and fetch your horse, I can take you to the Circle B."

"You're getting ahead of yourself," Fargo told him. The account made sense as far as it went but he still wasn't satisfied and he didn't lower the Henry. "Why does your boss want to see me?"

"To hire you. He says he is willing to pay you a thousand dollars to do him a favor."

Fargo whistled. "It must be some favor." He waited for the cowboy to tell him what it was but Stoddard just sat there. "Is it a secret or am I supposed to guess?"

"I would say if I knew. The boss wants to tell you himself. He did say that he'd give you a hundred dollars just to come hear him out."

"He's awful generous with his money."

"He can afford to be." Stoddard wagged his arms. "Can I put these down? My shoulders are commencing to hurt." He started to do it anyway and stiffened when Fargo sighted down the Henry's barrel. "Hold on. I just explained everything. You have no call to shoot me."

"People don't always tell the truth." Holding the Henry steady, Fargo moved to a lower branch. "Shed the hardware. Use two fingers."

"Damn, you are one suspicious son of a bitch," Stoddard complained, but he slowly plucked the revolver from its holster and slowly bent and let it drop to the grass. "Happy now?"

"Open the vest."

"All I've got under it is my shirt."

"Open it anyway."

Frowning, the cowboy parted the vest wide. "There. I'm not carrying a hideout. I'm no assassin. I punch cows for a living."

Still keeping the Henry on him, Fargo slipped to the lowest branch, perched for a moment with his legs dangling, and dropped. He landed in a crouch on the balls of his feet. Unfurling, he sidled around and picked up the Starr. "I'll hold on to this until I think I can trust you."

"I don't much like you taking my six-shooter. I feel half naked without it."

Fargo sympathized. He would feel the same. "Your boss should have told you what he wants me for. He must have plenty of cowhands working for him—"

"Pretty near thirty."

"Yet he needs me to do him a favor? Why not have one of you do it?"

"I honest to God don't know. The big sugar doesn't confide in me like he does Griff Jackson."

"Who?"

"The foreman. As tough an hombre who ever lived. If Mr. Bell had sent Jackson instead of me, he'd take your rifle and beat you half to death with it."

Fargo moved a few yards behind the cowboy's sorrel. "Ride ahead until we get to my horse. No tricks, hear?"

"Mister, I ain't featherheaded. I get forty a month, and found. That's hardly enough to die for."

Fargo was beginning to like him. "Why don't you tell me a little bit about yourself?"

"What the hell for?"

"To pass the time."

Stoddard muttered something, and then declared, "If this don't beat all. Are all of you Daniel Boones so nosy?"

"The ones who are fond of breathing."

"There's not much to tell. I was raised on a farm in Indiana. I got an itch and drifted west when I was sixteen and did some cow work and liked it. Been at it every since. Drifted to Denver a while back and Mr. Bell was hiring and I signed on."

"He came all the way up here to start a ranch?" Fargo had heard of a few but there wasn't a town to be had for hundreds of miles and no railhead, either.

"Mr. Bell ain't like you and me. He's always looking to the future. He says as how the country is growing and people are multiplying like rabbits and all of them will need beef to eat."

"He's not worried about Indians? The Bannocks or the Cheyenne or the Arapaho?" All of whom, Fargo knew, had clashed with whites in recent years.

The situation was bound to get worse now that the Indians realized the white man intended to claim their land.

"Mr. Bell says it will be a cold day in hell before he'll let redskins or anyone else run him—" Stoddard stopped and straightened and reined up. "Say, is that your animal?"

Fargo looked, and his blood chilled. They were almost to the spruce. The Ovaro was no longer tied to it. Three men were about to lead it away. Two were on horseback. The third had dismounted to untie the reins and had them in his hand. Fargo stalked toward them. He tossed the Starr to the cowpoke as he went by and snapped, "That's my horse you're stealing."

The three were cut from the same coarse cloth. They weren't white and they weren't red. They were a mix. Their clothes were grubby and they were grubby but their rifles and revolvers looked to be well oiled and their eyes glittered like the eyes of hungry wolves.

The man holding the stallion's reins had a Sharps at his side and bushy eyebrows as big as wooly caterpillars. "It was here by itself," he said. "We reckoned maybe someone left it."

Fargo almost called him a liar to his dirty face. Instead he held out his left hand. "I'll take those."

"Sure, mister." The breed held out the reins. "We don't want trouble. If you say it's yours, it's yours." He turned to climb on his mount.

"Hold on." Fargo was wondering how it was that they happened to be there at the same time as Jim Stoddard. He glanced at the cowboy and saw that Stoddard had holstered the revolver. "You didn't think to holler and see if anyone was around?"

The breed shrugged. "We figured anyone who would leave a fine animal like this must be dead. It's not as if we were following you to steal it."

"That's exactly what they were doing," Jim Stoddard remarked.

Both Fargo and the half-breed looked at him and said, "What?"

"I spotted them yesterday, south of you a ways," the puncher explained. "They were shadowing you and keeping well hid. It's why I rode hard to catch up today. I figured you'd want to know."

"Well, now." Fargo shifted so he could watch all three and said to the man who'd had the reins, "You're a liar as well as a horse thief."

"You're taking his word over mine? Why? Because he's a white and I'm not?"

"No. I'm taking his word because you were fixing to steal my horse, you goddamn idiot."

The man with the caterpillar eyebrows scowled. "I don't take kindly to insults," he said, and dropped his hand to his six-gun.

2

Fargo rammed the Henry's muzzle into the man's gut hard enough to double him over. Hissing through clenched teeth, the breed staggered and tried to draw. Fargo wasn't about to let him. He swung the Henry in a tight arc. There was the thud of the hardwood stock against the breed's head and then the thud of the man's unconscious form when he struck the ground. Instantly, Fargo leveled the Henry at the other two but it wasn't necessary.

Jim Stoddard had already drawn and was covering them. "I don't like to see anyone shot in the back."

"I'm obliged." Fargo relieved the man he had knocked out of his hardware, then did the same with the two still on their mounts. "Climb down," he commanded.

"What for?" the scrawniest of them asked.

Fargo motioned. "Sling him over his horse and get the hell out of here."

"You're letting us live?"

By rights Fargo was justified in blowing them from the saddle. He was sure they were horse thieves but there was always the chance, however slight, that they were telling the truth. "I can remedy that if you're disappointed."

"We'll do as you want."

The pair glared at Fargo at they lifted and hoisted. Then they swung back up and the scrawny one said, "You shouldn't ought to have done that to Speckled Wolf. When he comes around he'll be madder than a wet hen and out for your blood."

"He'll have a hard time blowing out my wick without his guns."

"That won't stop us. We can always get more." The scrawny man reined around.

"Speckled Wolf won't let you do it," the third breed said.

"Won't let me do what?" Fargo asked, but the pair was departing with their unconscious friend dangling limp like so much wet wash.

"What the hell was that all about?" Fargo wondered.

"Who can say with breeds?" Jim Stoddard said. "They're all half loco."

"They are no different than you or me." Fargo didn't take his eyes off them.

They might have concealed weapons and take it into their heads to come back and try to do him in.

"Are you an Injun lover?" the cowboy asked.

"They're people like everyone else."

"That must come from living with them," Stoddard said. "I hear tell a lot of your kind do."

"My kind?"

"Plainsmen. Scouts. Whatever you call yourself. A lot of them live with Injuns and take up Injun ways and before you know it are part Injun themselves."

"You make it sound like a disease," Fargo observed.

"I don't much care about redskins. But so long as they leave me be, I leave them be." Stoddard chuckled. "Mr. Bell says there will come a time when the tribes will rise up and try to drive us out. Do you believe that will happen?"

"It wouldn't surprise me any." Although Fargo hoped it never came to that. He had as many red friends as white.

"The prairie and the mountains will run hip deep in blood, was how Mr. Bell put it," Stoddard said.

"You put a lot of stock in what he says."

"You will too once you meet him," Stoddard predicted.

"He's awful smart. He went to school until he was near twenty and he reads books and everything."

The three would-be horse thieves were almost out of sight. Fargo felt safe in lowering the Henry and gathering up their weapons. He put their pistols in his saddlebags and slid their rifles into his bedroll and retied the bedroll. As he climbed on the Ovaro he caught the cowboy studying him. "Something on your mind?"

"I'm a mite surprised you didn't shoot the one who went for his six-gun. I would have."

"I'm surprised myself," Fargo said.

"Why didn't you then? Any court in the land would hang him for what he did. You let him off easy."

Fargo shrugged. "I can't rightly say." He wanted to drop the subject but the cowpoke had more to say.

"You're not one of those live and let live gents, are you? I'd as soon know now so if we're attacked I know whether I can depend on you or have to do all the killing myself."

"If it comes to that I'll do my share," Fargo promised.

"Good. There is nothing more worthless in a shooting affray than a man who won't shoot."

Fargo let Stoddard lead. He'd rather have the cowboy's back to him than his back to the cowboy.

A day and a half of beeline travel brought them to Sweetwater Station. It consisted of the stage relay and a corral, a log saloon and three cabins. They rode in just as the sun was going down. Fargo thought it a good idea to stay the night and head out at first light.

"Oh? Didn't I tell you?" Stoddard said. "Mr. Bell figured it would be quicker and easier for you to meet him here. He's waiting for us." The cowboy nodded at a hitch rail. "That's his bay yonder. He should be in the saloon."

Fargo alighted and wrapped the reins around the rail. He strolled in and over to the bar and gave it a hard thump to get the bartender's attention.

The barkeep was as wide as a Conestoga and wore an apron

that had never been cleaned. He set a bottle of whiskey in front of Fargo, and pointed. "That gent there said you'd be back and he was right."

Most ranchers Fargo had met were brawny blocks of muscle bronzed by the sun. The man eating steak and potatoes at a corner table was a pale mouse in a brown suit with spectacles on the tip of his nose. He looked up as Jim Stoddard brought Fargo over.

"Took you long enough."

The cowboy colored slightly. "He hardly ever stops. I was in the saddle pretty near fifteen hours of the day."

Clarence Bell shifted his mouse-brown eyes to Fargo. "Have a seat and I'll tell you what you're to do."

Fargo swigged a mouthful and smacked his lips. "Mister, if you were any more full of yourself, your head would be as big as a melon. I'll take the hundred and I'll listen to what you have to say but that's as far as it goes."

"Fair enough." Bell indicated a chair. Stoddard went to sit in another but the rancher said, "Wait at the bar. This doesn't concern you."

"Whatever you say, Mr. Bell."

Fargo stretched out his legs and upended the bottle. The coffin varnish burned clear down to his gut. "You sure have him well trained."

"Any man who works for me does as I want him to do or he can seek employment elsewhere." Bell set down his fork and knife and adjusted his spectacles. "We've gotten off to a bad start. That's my fault. I took it for granted that you wouldn't have come back unless you wanted the job."

"Your puncher didn't know what the job is."

Clarence Bell sat back and made a tepee of his hands. "I read the newspapers, Mr. Fargo. I know a few things about you. For instance, you're considered one of the best scouts on the frontier. You've lived with Indians and fought Indians and know their way of life better than just about any white man alive."

"This job has something to do with them?"

"I'll get to that in a moment." Bell paused. "I've also read that you are a keen judge of horseflesh. That you, in fact, ride as fine an animal as can be found. A type of pinto that those who know horses call an Overo or an Ovaro. Am I correct?"

"In all that reading you did, did you come across the fact that I'm fond of fillies, red-eye, and poker?"

Bell smiled. "Your vices did merit mention, yes. But it is your affinity with Indians and horses that make you ideal for what I have in mind."

Fargo swallowed and felt himself relaxing. "I'm listening. Just don't get long-winded."

"You are a man who likes to get to the point. So am I." Bell removed his spectacles and held them toward the window. He took out a handkerchief and wiped them and put them back on. "My business acumen, I can immodestly boast, is second to—"

"Whoa there, hoss," Fargo interrupted. "Spare me the fifty-cent words. You have something to say, you say it plain."

"Very well," Bell smirked. "I am good at business. My instincts have led me to start one of the first ranches in the territory. I've brought in a few hundred head and intend to bring in thousands more. But cows are only part of it. I'd also like to breed horses. Not just any horses. The finest to be had anywhere." His smirk widened. "The finer they are, the more money in my pocket. Follow me so far?"

"Just because talking dictionaries annoy me doesn't make me dumb," Fargo said.

"My apologies. No insult was intended. If you don't mind my saying, you are a prickly individual."

"The point of all this?"

"To make my cattle herds the best they can be I am bringing in cattle from as far away as Texas. To make my horses the best they can be, I must bring in horses from far away, too." Bell placed his elbows on the table and leaned forward. "I want to be the first white man to own and breed Appaloosas."

13

Fargo turned to stone with the bottle almost to his mouth.

"You heard right," Bell declared. "Appaloosas. That means I must send someone to the Nez Perce. Now do you see where you fit in?"

Fargo lowered the bottle to his lap. The Nez Perce were widely regarded as some of the best horse breeders west of the Mississippi. The Comanches also prided themselves on fine horses but the Nez Perce bred a type of horse no one else did, a horse so exceptional that many would give anything to own one: Appaloosas.

The Palouse Horse some called them. Exactly when the Nez Perce started breeding them, no one could say. But it was well known that for years now the Nez Perce had been winnowing out unwanted traits by gelding inferior animals and mating the best strains.

"What do you think of my idea, sir?"

Fargo regarded Clarence Bell with a smidgen of new-found respect. "It's a fine notion. But the Nez Perce might not like the idea of a white man breeding their horses."

"You are familiar with the tribe, I take it?"

"I've been to their country a few times, yes."

"Excellent." Bell excitedly rubbed his palms together. "Then you are just the man to go to them and offer whatever it will take on my behalf to buy the best Appaloosas they have."

Fargo sat back. It was a long ride to Nez Perce country, ten days to two weeks through rugged country wandered by hostiles and home to grizzlies and other beasts. "How high are you willing to go?"

"Didn't Jim Stoddard tell you? I will pay you a thousand dollars for your services, half in advance if you would like."

"No," Fargo said. "I meant how high for the Appaloosas?"

"Oh. Money is no object. I am quite wealthy. But just so they know I am in earnest, I authorize you to offer them five thousand dollars."

Fargo nearly fell out of his chair. "For *one* Appaloosa?"

"Of course not. I need two to breed. Five thousand dollars for a stallion and a mare. Do you think that's reasonable?"

"Hell, it's more than reasonable," Fargo said, and then was struck by a troubling thought. "You want me to tote that much money to Nez Perce country in my saddlebags?" If word got out, he'd be the target of every badman and greedy bastard in the territory.

"What do you take me for? I'll give you a thousand dollars to give to them as a token of my sincerity. The rest they can have when they bring the horses to me at the Circle B."

"Two thousand," Fargo said.

"I beg your pardon?"

"You want me to go all the way to Nez Perce country, talk them into parting with two of their best animals, then bring those animals all the way back. It will cost you two thousand or you can find someone else."

Bell's thin lips twitched. "You're taking advantage of the fact I need you. I resent that, sir."

"Resent it all you want. It's my hide. And it will take at least a month. Two thousand isn't asking so much considering how much you stand to gain."

The rancher drummed his fingers on the table. "Tell me. Is it true you are good friends with a Nez Perce chief?"

"His name is Gray Bear. I saved his son a while back and he's been grateful ever since." Fargo cocked his head. "You didn't read that in any newspaper."

"No, I did not. I heard it from an army captain. I've asked around about you, you see. I needed someone the Nez Perce would trust. I needed someone that *I* could trust. You would do the same in my shoes."

Fargo grunted.

Bell sat up. "Very well. Seeing as how you are exactly the man for the job, and seeing as how I need the two Appaloosas more than I have ever needed anything, I'm willing to pay you two thousand dollars for your services. But I'll still only pay you five hundred in advance. I give you a thousand, you might take it into your head to take my money and go on to San Francisco or someplace else and squander it gambling and whoring."

Fargo resented the insult. "When I give my word," he said harshly, "I keep it."

"So I've heard. Yet another of your attributes that persuaded me to offer you the job. What do you say? Do we have an accord? Will you go to the Nez Perce for me and bring back two horses?"

Fargo thought of his nearly empty poke.

"Well?" Bell impatiently prodded. "Don't keep me in suspense. Is it yes or is it no?"

"It's yes," Skye Fargo said.

3

Fargo was four days out of Sweetwater Station when he ran into trouble.

He was crossing a valley lush with grass and wildflowers. A goldfinch and its mate flew past. A meadowlark called. The sun was bright and warm, the day as perfect as a day could be.

A pungent scent tingled Fargo's nose. A scent that surprised him, given its source. He rose in the stirrups to see over the grass just as a rumbling snort heralded the rise of a behemoth from out of the very earth. Instantly, Fargo drew rein.

Back during the beaver trade the mountains had been home to a brute seldom seen now. The beaver men and those who came after had killed most of them off. Most, but not all. On occasion Fargo came across one, and he never knew how they would react. They were as unpredictable as bears and every bit as dangerous.

Mountain buffalo were shaggier than their prairie cousins. Shaggier and leaner although they stood as high at the shoulders—nearly six feet—and their curved horns were just as wicked. This one was a bull. It had been lying in a wallow, and the odor Fargo had smelled was its urine.

To make a wallow, buffalo gouged out clods of grass to expose the bare dirt and then urinated and rolled on their backs to cake themselves in mud, all in an effort to ward off the hordes of insects that plagued them.

The bull snorted and pawed the ground and tossed its head, its dark eyes fixed intently on Fargo and the Ovaro.

Fargo hoped to God it wouldn't charge. His Henry was in the saddle scabbard and the Colt would be next to useless. Besides which, he didn't want to kill it if he could help it. He had no need of the meat and couldn't afford the time to cure the hide. All he could do was sit quiet and wait for the buffalo to make up its mind.

Then the grass to his right moved and out stepped a cow. She wasn't as agitated as her mate. All she did was stare.

The Ovaro, thankfully, didn't whinny or shy. The slightest movement, the slightest sound, might provoke an attack.

Unexpectedly, the grass moved a third time, and from behind the cow pranced a calf. It came straight toward the stallion.

Inwardly, Fargo swore. Should the cow or the bull perceive him as a threat to their young, they would be on him in a flying fury. To his consternation the calf came up to the Ovaro and eyed it quizzically.

The bull and the cow came closer, too, the bull continuing to rumble in irritation. Fargo gripped the reins with both hands and tensed to use his spurs. If he reined away quickly enough and if the bull and the cow were slow in coming after him, he might get away.

The calf playfully skipped about the stallion, its tail bobbing, and uttered a short bleat. Unconcerned, it moved off into the high grass, and in a few seconds its mother followed. The bull gave a last snort and lumbered after its family, not once taking its eyes off the intruders.

Fargo let out a long breath, and laughed. Moments like these were the spice that made the wilds so appealing. He liked the new, the unexpected, life on the razor's edge. The humdrum of city life wasn't for him.

On Fargo rode. About four in the afternoon he shot a rabbit. Toward sunset he stopped for the night below the crest of a high ridge. It sheltered him from the wind and gave him an unobstructed view of his back trail for many miles. He gathered fallen branches and got a fire going. After putting coffee on to boil, he drew his Arkansas toothpick from its ankle sheath, skinned the rabbit, and cut the meat into chunks. He sharpened the end of a long stick, skewered several pieces, and held them to the flames.

The aroma made his mouth water. Once the outside of the meat was brown, he tore into the first piece with relish. About to take another bite, he checked his back trail and stiffened.

Far to the southeast a pinpoint of light had flared.

It could be anyone, Fargo reflected. The trail he was following was used by Indians, and others. It could also be someone following him. He would find out soon enough. For now he was content to sit back and enjoy his meal.

A wolf howled and was answered by another. An owl hooted, and wings fluttered in the dark.

Fargo patted the poke under his shirt, now bulging with five hundred dollars. As soon as he was done with this business with the Appaloosas, he aimed to head for Denver and treat himself to a week or two of perfumed ladies and smoke-filled saloons.

In a little while he turned in. He slept fitfully, waking up at the slightest little sound, which wasn't like him. Toward daybreak he decided enough was enough and got up and put the coffeepot on.

Shortly before dawn a speck of orange appeared to the southeast. Whoever it was, they were up early as well.

Two days went by. Two days without incident. Fargo stopped as often as the Ovaro needed rest. At night he listened to the wolves and the coyotes and stared at the spot of orange that always appeared. Whoever was back there wasn't trying to overtake him, which was encouraging.

By now Fargo was deep in the mountains. So deep, few white men had ever been there. He figured it would be another five days before he was in Nez Perce territory.

Finding one of their villages might take some doing. The tribe moved with the seasons and the food supply, and at that time of the year, could be found along the Clearwater, Salmon and Snake rivers. They fished as much as they hunted and were particularly fond of salmon.

They didn't call themselves the Nez Perce. The name was bestowed on them by the French. It meant "pierced nose." Ironically, it was a practice they seldom indulged in. The French had got them confused with another tribe and the name stuck.

That happened a lot. Whites rarely called tribes by their real names.

The Shis-Inday were known as Apaches. The Shoshones were called Snakes. The Lakotas were called Sioux. The Absarokes were known as Crows. The Siksika were commonly called Blackfeet. Tribe after tribe it was always the same.

The Nez Perce called themselves the Nimipuu, their word for "the people." They were a proud, strong tribe, protective of their territory, fierce to their enemies.

Fargo was fortunate in having befriended them. He was one of the few whites they trusted.

All this was going through his mind as he wound down a switchback. He glanced at the narrow valley below and promptly drew rein. A line of riders was coming down the valley in his direction. He didn't think they had spotted him. Their lances and shields told him they weren't white men. But he couldn't tell if they were friendly or hostile.

Fargo reined into the trees. He had counted nine warriors, more than enough to help themselves to his hair. Dismounting, he moved to the forest's edge. He was hoping the warriors would ascend the mountain by a different route, but there they were, climbing toward the switchback. They were bound to spot the Ovaro's tracks.

"Damn." Fargo ran to the stallion and swung back on. He reined deeper into the woods and after half a mile swung toward the valley floor. He hadn't gone far when the Ovaro pricked its ears and looked behind them.

Up above, men and horses were winding among the boles.

The warriors were after him.

Fargo still couldn't see them clearly enough to tell if they were Nez Perce.

To let them get closer invited an arrow in the ribs so he did the only thing he could—he fled.

The woods were thick but there were few downed logs or deadfalls to worry about. Fargo resorted to his spurs but didn't bring the Ovaro to a gallop until he came to the valley floor.

A war whoop pierced the air. The first of his pursuers had emerged from the trees, a dusky painted warrior who waved a bow overhead and then gave chase.

Others were strung out after him.

At last Fargo could see them clearly. They weren't Nez Perce. They were Blackfeet. Bitter enemies of the Nez Perce and whites alike, they often raided Nez Perce territory to lift hair and steal Appaloosas. To the Blackfeet, stealing a horse was considered as high a coup as taking an enemy's life.

This was the last thing Fargo needed. He stuck to the open valley for as long as he could. The Ovaro gained but not enough to be sure of escaping their painted pursuers. Fargo had hard riding ahead.

The valley came to an end at the bottom of a steep slope. Pines and spruce gave way to rows of firs. Fargo glanced back just as a whizzing shaft thudded into a tree. Hunching low, he zigzagged.

Higher up it was open save for scattered boulders and rock formations.

A cluster of slabs gave Fargo inspiration. Reining behind them, he vaulted down and yanked the Henry from the saddle scabbard. Quickly, he ran to the lowest slab and jammed the rifle to his shoulder.

The Blackfeet were climbing swiftly. Three warriors were out ahead of the others, two armed with bows and the third with a lance. Fargo banged off a shot. He deliberately fired over their heads as a warning. Kill one, and it would only make the rest more determined.

The three looked up but didn't slow or stop. One of the warriors drew a bowstring to his cheek and let fly. The arrow fell short but not by much.

Fargo fixed a bead, held his breath to steady his aim, and smoothly stroked the trigger. The Henry boomed and bucked and down the slope the bowman clutched at his chest and pitched from his mount. The other two drew rein.

Counting on that to delay them, Fargo ran to the Ovaro, shoved the Henry into the scabbard, and forked leather. He continued up the mountain until he came to a gap that would take him into the next valley. Stopping, he patted the Ovaro's sweaty neck and glanced down.

The war party was still after him.

"Damn it." Fargo went through the gap and descended into heavy timber. He was in for a long chase unless he could think of a way to throw them off. After a quarter of a mile he reined parallel to the valley floor and stayed in the trees where he would be harder to spot. He had gone a short way when he came to where part of a slope had given way, possibly from heavy rain, and scores of trees had fallen. The jumble of logs gave him an idea.

The deadfall covered about five acres. Fargo rode to the far end and then up and around to where it began. Dismounting, he moved out onto the logs. They were of all sizes. He had to be careful. One slip and he would fall in among them. Leaping from log to log he came to one that suited his purpose. It was precariously balanced on top of the others. Could he budge it? Lying flat on a different log, he placed his boots flat against it and pushed with all his might. The log moved but only an inch or so. Gritting his teeth Fargo tried again. For long seconds nothing happened. His sinews weren't equal to his need. Then the log started to roll. Instantly, he stopped and sat up. He was ready.

Presently the Blackfeet appeared. They were following his tracks and when they came to the deadfall they rode along the bottom as he had done. It never occurred to them that he might be up on the logs; no one in their right mind climbed onto deadfalls.

Fargo marked the distance. Lying on his back again, he put his boots to the log and strained with all his might. The log refused to move. He tried again, every muscle corded tight. The log began to roll. Another moment, and gravity took over. The log he had pushed rolled onto the next log and dislodged it and both rolled against others and dislodged some of them. Like snow gathering size and speed in an avalanche, the tumbling logs multiplied.

Down below, the Blackfeet had drawn rein in startled amazement. Realizing their peril, they reined around and flew for their lives. Only some made it. Others were engulfed in a crashing whirl of rolling timber. Their cries and the whinnies of their mounts betokened their fate.

Fargo hurried to the Ovaro and resumed his flight. When he had gone over a mile he stopped so the stallion could rest. For half an hour he watched his back trail. No one showed. The Blackfeet had apparently decided he wasn't worth the effort. Chuckling at how clever he had been, he rode on.

Fargo opened his saddlebags, took out a piece of pemmican, and nibbled. He had been lucky. One day his luck would play out and his bleached bones would be added to the legion the wild had already claimed. Until then, he would live as he pleased and do as he pleased, and when his time came, he would leave the world with no regrets.

That evening he camped on a sparsely treed slope. He made a small fire and used the last of the water in his canteen to make coffee. Tomorrow he would refill it. There were plenty of streams thereabouts. Plenty of game, too.

He filled his battered tin cup with the piping-hot brew and held it in his palms, and sipped. Stars had blossomed, sparkling like so many gems in a sea of ink. Wolves and coyotes began their nighttime chorus punctuated by the cries and roars of other creatures.

Fargo smiled. This was the life. The life he could no more

do without than he could do without his heart or his lungs. He finished the cup and poured another. Two was his limit. Any more and he might have trouble sleeping.

A meteor blazed the heavens.

Down below, the panicked cry of a rabbit was silenced by the snarl of a bobcat.

Prey and predator, the unending cycle. To Fargo, it was as ordinary as air. He had gotten so used to it that when a grizzly roared he paid it no mind. The bear wasn't near enough to pose a threat.

Fargo finished the cup and set it down. He leaned back on his saddle and laced his fingers behind his head. From the fire came the loud pop of a glazing red limb. It almost drowned out the stealthy pad of a footstep.

Fargo spun.

Stalking toward him was a Blackfoot warrior with a knife and a war club.

4

The instant their eyes met, the Blackfoot shrieked and launched himself over the flames.

It was rare for Fargo to be taken by surprise, rarer still that anyone could sneak up on him without him being aware. For a fraction of a second he was rooted in disbelief, and the warrior was on him. He grabbed the warrior's wrists but the tip of the knife sliced into his shoulder. Not deep, but it drew blood and his shoulder spiked with pain. They struggled, the warrior hissing through clenched teeth, Fargo striving his utmost to keep the knife from sinking into him and to keep the war club from slamming against his head.

The Blackfoot was immensely strong. He was in his middle years, a seasoned warrior. He wore his hair in braids and had on a buckskin shirt and leggings. His dark eyes glittered with grim intent as he put all his weight on his knife arm.

The razor edge dipped lower.

Driving his knee up, Fargo was rewarded with a wince and a guttural grunt. He drove his knee up again but the warrior shifted. The knife was a whisker's width from burying itself.

In desperation Fargo rammed his forehead against the Blackfoot's face. The warrior jerked back, blood streaming. Fargo kicked with both boots and the warrior was sent staggering into the fire.

A bound carried the Blackfoot clear. Shaking his head to

clear it, he growled like an enraged beast, and leaped to the attack.

This time Fargo was ready. Like a bolt of lightning, out flashed his Colt.

He fired and the warrior was jolted but kept coming and he fired again and a third time when the Blackfoot was almost on top of him. The war club swept on high to smash his skull. Fargo rolled. He made it clear just as the body of the warrior crashed to the ground.

Fargo turned, expecting to sell his life dearly. Where there was one warrior, there must be more. But no others came at him from out of the darkness. No war cries split the night.

It was several minutes before Fargo accepted that the dead warrior was the only one. He speculated that maybe the man had been sent on ahead to track him down. Or maybe the warrior had another reason.

Debating whether to stay where he was or move on, Fargo reloaded. The sound of a shot could carry a long way, especially when the wind was right. If the other warriors heard, they would come on hard and fast. He decided to find another spot to camp.

By three in the morning he was so tired he could barely keep his eyes open but he had put more miles between him and the Blackfeet. He was inclined to push on all night but the Ovaro needed to rest. This time he made a cold camp.

No sooner was he bundled in his blankets than he was out to the world. He slept until the shriek of a jay woke him shortly before dawn. Saddling the stallion, he pushed on. Two ridges and three valleys later he was fairly convinced he had outdistanced the war party and was safe.

The next several days were uneventful.

Then came the afternoon Fargo shot a grouse. He plucked it and rigged a spit over the fire and was sitting down to wait for it to roast when the Ovaro nickered.

Half a dozen warriors had materialized out of the greenery.

Fargo swooped his hand to his Colt but he didn't draw. Four of the six were riding Appaloosas. He smiled and raised his right hand to his neck, palm out. Extending his first two fingers, he raised his hand until his fingers were in front of his nose. It was sign language for "friend."

The Nez Perce approached. The youngest beamed broadly and when he drew rein he said in passable English, "My heart happy at see you again."

"Small Badger," Fargo said warmly. "Just the gent I've been hoping to run into."

"You want to run me?"

Fargo grinned. He knew that his young friend had learned English from a missionary and tried his best to speak it well. "I figured your band is usually hereabouts at this time of year." He motioned. "You and your friends are welcome to join me."

Small Badger slid down. He was dressed in a fringed buckskin shirt trimmed with red cloth. His hair hung in thick braids past each ear. In front, he had cropped his bangs above his eyebrows. On his back hung a quiver filled with arrows and a bow made from the horn of a mountain sheep. He offered his hand, white fashion. "You looking for me?"

Over the meal Fargo explained why he was there. His young friend listened with interest.

"Five thousand much money, yes?"

"A small fortune to whites," Fargo remarked, especially as most were lucky to earn four hundred a year.

"You must ask father," Small Badger said. "Him decide."

Fargo had reckoned as much. The Nez Perce were choosy about who they sold their horses to. They didn't want Appaloosas to fall into the hands of enemies like the Blackfeet.

"It good you come." Small Badger clapped him on the shoulder. "Gray Bear be happy see you."

Fargo hoped so, or he had ridden all that way for nothing. In his mind's eye he flashed back to the day he saved Small Badger from whites out to hang him for something he didn't

27

do. To the Nez Perce way of thinking, that put them in his debt.

"Father not same man," Small Badger said.

"How do you mean?"

"One day Bloods come, try steal horses. My father and others fight them. Father shot with arrow here." Small Badger touched his leg. "Him pull out but now father like this." Small Badger got up and limped in a circle.

"I'm sorry to hear that."

"Father not smile much. Make Mother sad. Make me sad."

Fargo remembered Gray Bear as being outgoing and friendly. "Some men get that way when they're scarred for life. I almost took an arrow myself on my way here."

"Who try shoot you?"

Fargo related his run-in with the war party. Small Badger became excited and was all for mounting up and going at them.

"There are more of them than there are of you," Fargo admonished. "Your best bet is to let them be. Sooner or later they'll drift back to where they came from."

"How many Nimipuu they kill before they go?" Small Badger shook his head. "Blackfeet our enemy. They too close our land. We must find. We must drive off or kill."

The other warriors listened to the chief's son translate and all were in agreement.

Fargo tried to talk them out of it. He would have to go with them and that would delay him. "I just want to buy a couple of horses and be on my way."

"I take you my father when Blackfeet dead or gone."

"I tangled with them days ago. They're probably halfway home by now."

"We not know that," Small Badger stubbornly insisted. "They be danger to my people. I warrior now. I must protect them. Must drive enemy off."

Fargo was sorry he had brought it up. Later, after the Nez Perce turned in, he lay racking his brain for a way to change

Small Badger's mind. The chief wouldn't take it kindly if his son was killed, and would likely as not blame him.

The next morning Fargo tried again but he wasted his breath. The six Nez Perce checked their bowstrings and sharpened their knives and tomahawks, and were ready.

Reluctantly, Fargo retraced his back trail. He seldom rode faster than a walk as much to spare their animals as in the hope that if he took long enough, the Blackfeet would be long gone and he could get on about the business that brought him there.

Small Badger stayed at his side. He had grown a couple of inches since Fargo saw him last but in one respect the young warrior hadn't changed a lick; he loved to gab. "I glad you come. We blood brothers for life."

"I'm fond of you, too," Fargo allowed, and meant it. The young warrior was so earnest and sincere it was hard *not* to like him.

"You remember name I give you?"

"How could I forget?" Fargo joked. "I still say it doesn't fit."

"I call you Iron Will because what you want, you get. When you make up mind, you do. You have strongest will I meet."

"If it was half as strong as you claimed, we wouldn't be doing what we're doing," Fargo said. "It's a mistake to court trouble when there's no need."

"I told you. Must make sure my people safe. You do same were you Nimipuu."

"I suppose."

"You find woman yet?"

Fargo looked at him. "Where the hell did that come from?"

"Pardon?"

"I'm not looking to get hitched in this life or any other. What made you ask such a thing?"

Small Badger grinned. "I remember how you like females. You like them more than eat. You like them more than sleep."

"Hell."

"Last time you come village you stay seven sleeps and lay with two women. My t'ot—sorry, my father—him say you have qoq'a lx in pants."

"I have what?"

"You be buffalo where most men goats. You understand?"

Fargo laughed. "I reckon I've never had a lady complain, at that. But you should keep it to yourself."

"Not tell anyone? Why?"

"White men like to pretend they don't have one."

His face scrunching in confusion, Small Badger asked, "That new word. What be 'pretend'?"

"It means you act as if it's not there."

"But it part of us, like arm and leg and head. Touch every day. How not be there when is there?"

"You're asking the wrong gent," Fargo told him. "I've never ignored mine." He chuckled. "How the hell did we get on this, anyhow?"

"You lay with women."

Fargo changed the subject. He asked how the Nez Perce were getting along with whites these days and learned that while they were still the friendliest tribe around except for the Shoshones, relations with white men had soured.

"Too many come our land," Small Badger complained. "Kill animals. Look for yellow rock in streams."

"Those rocks are worth a lot of money and most whites want to be rich more than they want to be anything."

"You want be rich too?"

Fargo shrugged. "I never gave it much thought. I like a full poke as much as the next gent but I can get by without one."

"This white who send you. This Bell. He must have much money."

"He has more than he knows what to do with," Fargo said. "Ten years from now, odds are he'll have even more."

"You think it good we let him have m'a mim?"

Fargo recalled that was Nimipuu for "Appaloosa." "I don't

see how it can hurt." Bell would only sell to whites, not to Nez Perce enemies.

"If you say it good, I ask father to help. We have much horses. Or should be many horses?"

"Much and many are about the same."

"I sorry I not well at white tongue. Words make my head in whirl. Whites not think like we think."

Just then one of the warriors behind them barked the Nez Perce word for "enemies," and pointed.

Half a mile away and half a mile lower down, warriors were winding along a valley toward them.

"We find Blackfeet!" Small Badger exclaimed, and was quick to rein into cover. The rest followed suit.

Fargo suspected it was the same war party he tangled with. If they continued the way they were, the Blackfeet would ride right into an ambush. He slid the Henry out and levered a cartridge into the chamber.

"Shiny rifle," Small Badger said, referring to the brass receiver. "Where your buffalo gun?"

Once, Fargo favored a Sharps. It was powerful enough to drop a buffalo with a single shot, but that was also the reason he switched; the Sharps held only one cartridge at a time. The Henry, on the other hand, held fifteen in a tubular magazine under the barrel. When a man was in a pinch and needed to spray a lot of lead, the Henry beat the Sharps all hollow.

The Nez Perce were notching arrows to their bowstrings and seeking spots to conceal themselves.

Fargo stayed close to Small Badger. When the young warrior squatted behind a pine, Fargo hunkered behind another right next to it. "It will be a while," he said.

Small Badger was practically squirming with excitement. "I count coup this day. I make my father proud."

"The Blackfeet are good fighters," Fargo reminded him.

"Nimipuu good fighters too."

The Nez Perce had to be. Their territory, abundant as it was with game and grass and water, was coveted by other tribes.

Any sign of weakness on their part and they would be driven off.

Small Badger tested his bowstring and gazed at the approaching Blackfeet. "It good day to die."

"I hope not," Skye Fargo said.

5

Skye Fargo had heard that expression before. It never made sense to him. He liked being alive. He liked how whiskey burned as it went down his throat, he liked the soft feel of a willing woman, he liked the delicious taste of a juicy steak. Dying put an end to all that, permanent. For him, there was no good day to die. Anyone who thought there was didn't appreciate breathing.

Soon the war party was near enough that Fargo could see how alert they were. They rode with their weapons at the ready; bows with arrows nocked, lances held to throw. They were cautious this near to enemy country.

"Wait until they are right on top of us," Fargo whispered. That way the Nez Perce would drop more with their first flight of arrows.

"I wait, Iron Will," Small Badger promised. He grinned and flexed his fingers and shifted his feet.

Fargo thought to ask, "Have you ever fought Blackfeet before?"

"No."

Fargo had another thought and it troubled him. "Tell me something. How many warriors have you counted coup on?"

"None."

"Hell." Fargo should have realized. Small Badger was young and eager to prove himself. The other warriors had gone along with him because he was a chief's son.

"What be wrong?" Small Badger whispered back.

"It's not too late to change your mind."

"Why I do that?" Small Badger raised his horn bow. "We kill enemies, women sing songs of us."

"Just what I've always wanted."

"Pardon?"

"Nothing. Pay attention to the Blackfeet. And whatever you do, stay behind that tree."

"Can't kill with knife from behind tree. Must get close to show have courage."

Fargo put his cheek to the Henry. He hoped to God they got through this. That was the trouble with spilling blood. Sometimes the blood that was spilled was your own.

Small Badger and the other Nez Perce had drawn their bowstrings back and were sighting down the shafts.

Fargo took aim on the fourth Blackfoot. He figured the Nez Perce would go for the closest.

"It good day to die," Small Badger said again, and let fly. The twang of his bowstring was the signal for the others to loose their shafts.

Fargo squeezed the trigger.

Three of the Blackfeet fell in the first volley but only two were dead. The third had been hit in the shoulder. Another was struck in the ribs but the arrow didn't penetrate deep and he was still on his horse. Now he and the remaining mounted warriors showed why the Blackfeet were so widely respected as fighters; they reined toward the woods, and charged.

Fargo jacked the lever and fixed a quick bead. A buckskin-clad chest filled his sights and he fired. At the boom the warrior was jolted but somehow stayed on his horse.

Arrows and lances flew thick. War whoops pierced the air. A Nez Perce went down, thrashing and kicking, a shaft through his throat. A spear transfixed another low in the side and a shower of scarlet erupted.

Then the Blackfeet were in among them and it was every man for himself. Fargo dived as a shaft sought his neck and it whizzed over his head. He rolled and came up with the

Henry level but the Blackfoot who loosed the arrow at him had taken an arrow from a Nez Perce. He spun to see how his young friend was faring.

Small Badger was down. Over him stood a Blackfoot with a war club raised on high.

Fargo fired, worked the lever, fired again. At each blast the Blackfoot was jarred back a step. Suddenly the man bellowed in rage and flew at him. Fargo got the Henry up in time to deflect a blow that would have caved in his head. He slammed the stock against the warrior but it had no effect. The war club scraped his shoulder. He ducked, sidestepped, and rammed the barrel into the Blackfoot's gut. It, too, had no effect.

In the savage heat of combat some men were immune to harm. Bloodlust overcame them and they went virtually berserk. This warrior swung his war club in a wild frenzy, seeking to batter the rifle aside and bring Fargo down.

Fargo backpedaled. He blocked a swing from up high and a sweep from down low and then he clipped the warrior on the cheek. All it did was make the Blackfoot madder. With another bellow, the Blackfoot leaped and brought the heavy war club smashing down. The Henry was torn from Fargo's grasp. Throwing himself clear, Fargo drew his Colt. He fired twice from the hip and he didn't miss.

In the abrupt silence, Fargo's ears rang. He looked around. All the Blackfeet were down but so were half the Nez Perce. The battle had been brutal and bloody. He turned toward Small Badger and his blood chilled in his veins.

"No."

The chief's son was still on his back, blood welling from a gash on his temple.

Fargo ran to him and knelt. He gripped Small Badger's wrist and felt for a pulse and was elated to find one, strong and steady. He examined the wound. The war club had glanced off, taking a lot of skin and flesh but doing no serious harm. He shook Small Badger's shoulder. Small Badger groaned. Fargo shook him again, harder.

The young warrior's eyelids fluttered. He opened his eyes and gazed groggily about him and said something in his own tongue.

"Do you know where you are?" Fargo asked.

"Iron Will?" Small Badger licked his lips. "I still live?"

"No thanks to the Blackfoot who tried to bash your brains out," Fargo said, and nodded at the fallen figure.

Rising onto his elbows, Small Badger grimaced. "Feel much sick between ears."

"You might have a concussion."

"What that?" Small Badger tried to raise a hand to his temple but sank down and groaned.

"It means you are hurt inside your head," Fargo explained it as simply as he could. "You must take it slow and easy for a while."

"Blackfeet all dead?"

"Every last one."

Small Badger smiled weakly. "Good. My father be proud. I protect my people."

"I hope the cost was worth it."

Lifting his head, Small Badger looked about. His smile changed to deep sorrow. "Otter Tail. Two Owls." He closed his eyes and sank back down. "They my friends."

"Not anymore," Fargo said. "They would still be alive if you hadn't wanted to fight the Blackfeet so much."

"Men do what must," Small Badger said. "Now Blackfeet no raid village. They die good."

The wounded were tended to. The dead Blackfeet were stripped of weapons, their horses collected. The Nez Perce left the hair of the Blackfeet untouched.

Unlike many other tribes, the Nez Perce took no pride in lifting scalps.

Fargo wanted to bandage Small Badger but the younger man wouldn't let him.

"Let people see wound. They know I brave."

Fargo sighed. "At least wash it." Dirt was in the gash and could lead to infection.

"I fine," Small Badger happily declared.

By late afternoon he had the chills and was swaying so badly he couldn't sit his horse. The other warriors called an early halt. A fire was kindled. Two warriors went off to hunt.

Fargo brought his bedroll over to where Small Badger lay curled on his side, his teeth chattering, his whole body shaking. Unrolling the blankets, he said, "Bundle yourself in these."

"They yours. I not need."

"You're too damn hardheaded for your own good." Taking hold of the young warrior's shoulders, Fargo hauled him onto the blankets.

Small Badger was so startled he didn't resist. Nor did he object when Fargo covered him. An hour later he was muttering and mumbling. An older warrior came over and put a hand on Small Badger's forehead. He motioned for Fargo to do the same. Small Badger was burning up.

Fargo had tried to warn him. Infected wounds killed more people than the guns and knives that caused the wounds.

The older warrior opened a pouch and showed Fargo the contents. In it were plantain leaves. He applied several directly to the wound and then ground others into a powder and mixed them with clematis leaves to make a tea that he forced Small Badger to drink.

Some whites scoffed at Indian remedies, but not Fargo. He had seen them work too many times. When he felt Small Badger's brow a couple of hours later the fever had broken. By morning it was gone and the young warrior awoke ravenous and eager to be on their way.

The others did not speak to Fargo unless he spoke to them first. They had won a hard fight and should be in fine spirits but they had lost two of their own. They were taking their slain friends back for burial and must hurry before the bodies began to decompose.

Their village lay beside a gurgling stream in a verdant valley. The lodges were similar to those of the Shoshones, Crows, and Sioux: buffalo hides stretched over frames of lodgepoles. Everyone in the village came running.

The wives of the dead warriors broke into wails of lament.

Gray Bear emerged from a sweat lodge to greet his son. He welcomed Fargo, listened to an account of the fight, and then called for a council for later. There were the burial preparations to attend to, and a victory to celebrate.

Everyone hurried off, leaving Fargo holding the Ovaro's reins. He decided to go to the stream and let the stallion drink, and turned.

"You have come back."

"Eapalekthiloom," Fargo said.

Her name meant "Many Clouds" in English. She wasn't much over five feet tall yet every inch was exquisite. Raven hair cascaded past her slender shoulders to the small of her back. Her ample bosom, her narrow waist, the shapely contours of her thighs—all were highlighted by her doeskin dress with its many blue and white beads. She spoke English better than Small Badger; better, even, than anyone in her band. Keen intelligence, and something else, were mirrored in her lovely eyes. "Iron Will. He Who Rides Many Trails. Skye Fargo. How would you be called?"

"However you want."

"You are not a man a woman forgets. I have thought of you often. I hoped that one day you would return to see me."

"I came to see Gray Bear."

"Oh." Many Clouds didn't hide her disappointment. "So you still ride where the wind takes you."

"Afraid so." Fargo motioned. "I'm on my way to the stream. You're welcome to tag along."

Many Clouds hesitated but only for a second. Falling into step beside him, her small hands clasped in front of her, she said softly, "It is not good for a woman to give her heart to a man who does not give his heart to her."

"We've been all through that. I never promised anything. I was honest with you."

"Yes, you always speak with a straight tongue," the beauty allowed. "How long are you staying?"

"It depends on Gray Bear."

"The night, at least?"

"At least," Fargo said.

Many Clouds smiled and her hand brushed his arm. "I offer you our lodge. My mother and father will not mind. They know I am fond of you."

"I don't want to impose." Nor did Fargo care to endure the stares of her parents. He did that the last time.

The water was clear and cold and tasted delicious. Fargo dried his hand on his pants and sat with his forearms over his knees. High grass screened them from the village.

Many Clouds sat so close to him, their legs brushed. She leaned back, her mounds thrusting against her dress, her full lips quirked. "They will be busy until the sun goes down."

"Who?" Fargo was thinking of the last time he was with her, and twitched below his belt.

"My people. The dead must be buried with their medicine bundles. Their women must mourn for twelve moons and then hold a giveaway."

Fargo was familiar with the custom, unique among the Nez Perce. "Will you go to see them buried?"

"It is for family. I thought I would keep you company." Many Clouds placed her hand on his. "If you do not mind."

"We are a lot alike, you and me."

"In what way? I am a woman, you are a man. I am Nimipuu, you are white. I want a husband. You do not want a wife."

"There is one thing we both want," Fargo said.

"I admit I often think of our nights together. They were special." Many Clouds leaned toward him and lowered her voice. "I know I can never have you but I can please you and you can please me."

"A gal after my own heart."

"I am after something," Many Clouds said, and slid her hand between his legs.

6

Some women didn't play female games. Some didn't pretend they weren't interested when they really were. Some liked to be with a man as much as Fargo liked to be with a woman and weren't shy about letting him know. He'd always admired them for being so honest.

Many Clouds was one of those women. The last time Fargo paid Gray Bear's village a visit, she had taken an immediate liking to him and before the night was over had treated him to her many charms.

When Clarence Bell proposed coming to the Nez Perce for a pair of Appaloosas, Fargo had thought of that night with Many Clouds. He wouldn't mind another. Now, seated on the bank with the warm sun on them and hidden from the village, he pulled her to him and molded his mouth to hers. She was everything he remembered: warm, soft, delectable. Kissing some women was like kissing molten sugar. Her breasts were hard against his chest. Her hand cupped him, and he felt himself grow as rigid as iron.

"You are the best kisser," Many Clouds said softly when they broke for breath. "I could kiss you all day."

"What's stopping you?"

Many Clouds nodded at the trail to the village. "Others might come to drink. It is best we are together where no one can see."

"Couples are together in lodges all the time," Fargo said.

"Under robes and blankets."

Fargo got up and untied his bedroll. He spread out the blankets and covered her and him from their ankles to their shoulders, then pressed against her until she was on her back and he was cushioned by her yielding body. "How does this suit you?"

Many Clouds smiled. "You must want me very much."

"It's been a while." Fargo hadn't been with a woman in almost three weeks, a long spell to go without.

"It has been longer since you were here last."

"Don't start." Fargo refused to be nagged. "It's up to you. Do I roll up my blankets?"

Many Clouds looked away and then back again. "It will always be yes. Even if I move into the lodge of a warrior, it will always be yes."

"I thought the Nez Perce don't like that sort of thing," Fargo mentioned. Jealous husbands were high on his list of things he could do without.

"That does not matter. I will always be willing to lie with you. Do you understand what I am saying?"

"I still have to go where the wind takes me."

"I will not ask more than you can give. But I will say only this once that I wish it was different."

Fargo eased onto his elbow. He suspected she was having second thoughts but she surprised him by fiercely pulling him to her and giving him a kiss he felt in his toes. She had a way of moving her lips as she kissed that sent delightful tingles shooting down his body. They kissed and kissed, all the while he explored her luscious form, running his hands from her bosom to her knees, sculpting her through the doeskin dress. He cupped a breast and squeezed and Many Clouds cooed softly. He kneaded her thighs and she squirmed in rising ardor. He licked her neck and nibbled her earlobe and she did the same to him.

A fish jumped in the stream. Nearby, the Ovaro cropped grass. A bee buzzed the blankets.

No one else had come down the trail. The Nimipuu were busy preparing for the burials.

Fargo gave himself over to his hunger. He hiked her dress and delved a hand under. Her skin was silky smooth and pleasantly warm. He slid his fingers over her perfect thighs to her nether mound. She was wet with need and moaned when he parted her nether lips. He rubbed her tiny knob and she arched her back and tried to devour his mouth with hers.

Fargo inserted a finger and stroked. He nearly gasped when her fingers enfolded his member. She had gotten his pants undone without him realizing.

"You like that," Many Clouds huskily taunted.

"And you like this," Fargo said, sliding a second finger into her.

"More than anything."

Here was a woman after Fargo's own heart. He pumped and she ground into him. For a while he drifted on a tide of carnal pleasure and then she gripped him and said, "Please. I want you in me. Now."

Fargo was on the brink. Willing himself not to explode, he parted her legs.

Another moment, he thrust in and up.

Many Mounds stifled an outcry. Her nails dug into his shoulder and her ankles locked behind him. "Yes. Oh, yes."

A splash Fargo took to be another fish. He rocked on his knees and she thrust to meet him. They went faster and harder until of a sudden Many Clouds opened her mouth wide and gushed. Fargo tried to hold off but he wanted it as much as she did. He exploded. The world swam, and together they coasted to an eventual stop and lay panting and sweaty and grinning.

"That was nice," Many Clouds said quietly.

Fargo grunted.

"Did you not think it was nice?"

"Very," Fargo said, wishing she wouldn't talk.

"The bear must think it was nice, too."

"Bear?" Fargo said sleepily. He thought she was joking but when he glanced over his shoulder a black bear was in the middle of the stream staring back at him.

"What the hell?" he blurted, and grabbed for his Colt.

"Do not shoot. If it was going to attack us it would have done so by now."

Fargo wasn't so sure. Bears were about the most unpredictable critters on God's green earth. This one was young, not more than a year or so old. Still, it had inches-long claws and sharp teeth and could kill as easily as a bear twice its size.

He curled his thumb around the Colt's hammer.

"See?" Many Clouds said.

The black bear had turned and was moving to the far bank. It climbed out, shook itself and sent drops flying, and gave them a last curious look before it melted into the forest.

"That was an omen," Many Clouds declared.

"That you need to take a bath?"

"You are poking fun, as whites say. But you do not see the world as my people do. For me that bear was a sign. This is the last time we will lie together."

"A while ago you said—"

Many Clouds put a finger to his lips. "I know what I said. But now I know different."

"It was a bear, for God's sake."

"You do not believe. That is fine for you. But do not insult me if I do. For me the world is more than what the eyes see and the ears hear."

Fargo rolled off her and onto his side. Some whites were the same. They saw everything as omens from above. To him, things happened, and that was that. "I'll be around a while in case you change your mind."

Many Clouds touched his cheek. "No. The bear has told us. It makes me sad that we will never touch again."

"Hell."

"Let me hold you and we will rest and then I must join my people." Many Clouds nuzzled against him.

Fargo stretched out on his back. Given how busy Gray Bear would be for the rest of the day, he might have to wait until tomorrow to bring up the subject of the Appaloosas. He closed his eyes, and the next thing he knew, Many Clouds was shaking him.

"We fell asleep. I must hurry."

Fargo rose onto his elbows. Judging by the sun, they had slept about an hour. She was smoothing her dress. Smiling, she bent and traced his chin with a finger. Then she turned and hastened up the path.

Sitting up, Fargo hitched at his pants. He rolled up his bedroll and tied it on the Ovaro. Climbing on, he rode back. Hardly anyone paid attention to him. They were bustling about like so many bees. He went through the lodges to the open valley beyond, where the horse herd, consisting of hundreds of Appaloosas and others, was being watched over by several boys. It was an important responsibility and they took it seriously. Two reined over and used sign language to ask what he wanted.

Fargo answered by holding his right hand at shoulder height, his palm out, his fingers up, and twisted his wrist quickly three times. It was the sign for "question." He asked which stallion and which mare were the best in the entire herd.

One of the boys signed that all Nez Perce horses were fine animals.

Fargo chuckled and asked which of the many fine animals the boy considered the finest.

The boy kneed his pony and beckoned. He wound among the horses and presently drew rein and pointed.

Fargo whistled in admiration. He was a keen judge of horseflesh, and the stallion the boy had picked was superb. Over fifteen hands high, it had black and white spots on a roan background. Each hoof had white stripes and its eyes were rimmed white. Its mane was dark, its tail had a natural arch. The pinnacle of breeding for endurance and speed, here was an animal any warrior would give anything to possess.

"Question," Fargo signed. "Who own horse?" He figured it must be a prominent warrior. There were rich and poor Indians just as there were rich and poor whites, and the richest Indians nearly always owned the best animals.

"Gray Bear."

A stroke of luck, Fargo reckoned. "Question. Horse have name?" Some tribes wouldn't think of giving a name to something they might have to eat. Other tribes regarded their horses as highly as they did people.

"Yes." The boy raised his hands to his shoulders and flapped them up and down.

Fargo was puzzled. "You call horse Bird?"

The boy laughed. He held his right hand down below his waist, his hand closed, then suddenly snapped his hand up and popped his finger out.

Fargo was more puzzled than ever. "You call horse Bird Fire?"

"No." The boy repeated the signs and then pointed at the sky.

Then Fargo remembered. When used together, the signs for "bird" and "fire" actually stood for Thunder Bird, a giant bird that Indian legend had it caused thunder. Or the signs might stand for thunder, itself. "Question. You call horse Thunder?"

The boy motioned impatiently and then bunched his fist, held it so his knuckles were to the ground, and made chopping or clomping motions.

At last Fargo understood. "You call horse Thunderhoof."

"Yes," the boy confirmed, and took him to see two others. Both were exceptional but neither compared to Thunderhoof.

Fargo asked the boy to point out the best mares and was shown four. Only two aroused Fargo's interest. Neither had names, and neither belonged to Gray Bear.

By then they were on the far side of the herd, near the end of the valley.

The boy started around rather than to go back through.

Fargo followed. It would be quicker. He glanced at the shadowed forest less than a hundred yards away and wasn't alarmed when he spied movement. A deer, he figured, or some other animal. Then a black silhouette reared against the green, a silhouette with two legs. This close to the village, Fargo took it to be a Nez Perce.

He started to turn toward the boy just as a rifle boomed and a slug whizzed past his ear.

Fargo threw himself from the saddle. On horseback he was an easy target. In the grass he'd be hard to spot and harder to hit. Slicking the Colt from his holster, he banged off a quick shot at puffs of gun smoke.

The boy had reined around in alarm. He let out a yell, nocked an arrow to his bowstring, and galloped toward the woods.

"No!" Fargo shouted.

The boy didn't heed. He jerked his bow up and drew the string back but before he could let the shaft fly the rifle boomed a second time and the top of the boy's head exploded. Like a disjointed doll he flopped from his mount.

Fargo whipped erect and fired twice at the silhouette and then dropped flat.

There was no answering shot. He crawled to the boy and parted the grass, and swore. Rolling onto his side, he plucked cartridges from his belt and reloaded.

Distant yells and the drum of hooves told him help was on the way but it would take them a minute to get there. In the meantime, he would be damned if he would let the killer get away.

Pumping his legs, Fargo zigzagged toward the trees. He was careful not to rise too high so he didn't share the boy's grisly fate.

No shots thundered.

Fargo was a stone's toss from the tree line when a horse nickered and the undergrowth crackled. He ran faster and rose and glimpsed not one but three figures on horseback, swiftly fleeing.

One of the riders glanced back.

Fargo stopped cold in his tracks. "It can't be," he blurted.

He raised the Colt but the vegetation swallowed them. Frustrated and bewildered, he hurried to reclaim the Ovaro.

Several boys and a pair of warriors had arrived and were hunched over the body of the slain horse guard. They straightened as Fargo came up and the huskiest of the men stepped in front of him and raised a hand for him to stop.

"I know who did this," Fargo said. "I need my horse so I can go after them." He went to walk on but the warrior pushed him, hard, and he nearly fell. "Damn it, let me by."

Fargo had no time for this. He went to go around but the other warrior had slipped behind him and seized his arms. "Let me go, damn it." He reckoned they must think he was to blame.

The next instant a knife was pressed to Fargo's throat.

7

His wrists hurt from the rope but otherwise Fargo felt fortunate to be alive.

He gazed through the opening at the top of the lodge and listened to a commotion outside. The sun had gone down and the sky was darkening. He rolled onto his back and sat up. His hat was next to him. With his arms bound behind him he couldn't very well put it on.

The flap parted. Gray Bear entered and came over and sat cross-legged.

Small Badger kindled the fire and moved next to his father.

"How you be, friend?"

"Hungry," Fargo said.

Gray Bear went on at some length in the Nez Perce tongue. His son listened attentively, and then translated.

"My father come from council. Some warriors think you shoot Running Elk."

"I tried to tell them," Fargo said. "It wasn't me. It was someone in the trees."

"Warriors only see you. They say they hear shot and ride fast and find body and you come out of woods."

"The killer was already gone." Fargo had tried to explain but the two warriors who took him captive didn't speak English. He would have explained in sign but they had tied him up and angrily hustled him to this lodge and thrown him in and left.

"You see Running Elk's killer?"

"I caught a glimpse."

"Was it Blackfoot? Or maybe Sioux? Nimipuu have many enemies," Small Badger said.

"I didn't get a good enough look," Fargo lied. The Nez Perce wouldn't take kindly to the truth; namely, that Running Elk had been slain by a man out to kill him.

Gray Bear spoke and once more his son served as interpreter. "My father want know why you were at horses?"

"Didn't you tell him I came here to buy a couple of Appaloosas?"

"Not yet, no. I sorry. I busy other things." Small Badger talked to his father at considerable length and the chief replied.

"He say it strange you want m'a min and someone kill horse guard."

M'a min was the Nez Perce word for their famous breed. "Ask him to have someone go look in the trees. They'll find sign. It will prove I am telling the truth."

Gray Bear called out. The flap moved and a warrior poked his head inside.

Gray Bear said something and the warrior promptly ducked out again.

"Father do as you want. He send men to where Running Elk shot."

"Tell him I'm obliged."

Father and son talked, and Small Badger said, "Who this white man you want buy horses for?"

Fargo told them about Clarence Bell. He left nothing out. It was obvious the chief wasn't happy about the idea, and the first question Gray Bear posed through his son confirmed it.

"What we need with money? We trade for things we need."

"This white man is offering enough to buy guns and steel knives for every warrior and blankets and pots and pans for every woman," Fargo mentioned. "All for a stallion and a mare."

Small Badger translated.

Gray Bear bowed his head and was silent for a while. Finally he looked Fargo in the eyes and began a speech.

"Father say what you ask no white man ever ask before. Other tribes want breed our horses but we only trade geldings. We keep stallions. Only Nimipuu breed m'a min."

Fargo had expected this.

"M'a min . . . what is word?" Small Badger scratched his hairless chin. "M'a min special to Nimipuu. We breed many winters to make strong, make fast, make best horse we can."

"So the answer is no?"

Small Badger put the question to his father. "Him say he must think. It big thing, what you ask."

Fargo appreciated as much, and said so, adding, "Tell your pa not to base his decision on me. It doesn't matter to me if the man gets his horses. Say no and there will be no hard feelings."

"We still be friends?"

"If you want to be."

The young warrior clasped Fargo's arm. "You save me. You stop other whites from . . . how you say it?"

"Stringing you up by the neck."

"Yes. Stringing me. You and I be friends all time," Small Badger said sincerely.

The two left.

Fargo lay near the fire and pondered. It would be easy to escape. A few strokes of the Arkansas toothpick hidden in his boot, and all he had to do was find the Ovaro and light a shuck. But he could forget the Appaloosas. It would also cost him Small Badger's and Gray Bear's friendship. He elected to stay put.

The fire had burned low when the flap parted again and in came his friends.

"Father say tell you warriors find tracks," Small Badger reported.

"Man climb on horse then ride fast. Him join two others."

"There were three of them?" Fargo feigned surprise.

"We know you not shoot Running Elk."

Fargo shifted and wagged his bound wrists. "Cut me free and I'll go after the bastards."

"Not yours to do," Small Badger said. "Them kill Nimipuu. Nimipuu go after them. Nimipuu catch them. Nimipuu kill them."

"Let me help." Fargo had a personal reason that he wasn't about to share. "I'm a fair hand at tracking."

Small Badger passed on the request. "Father say him let you know." He began prying at the knots. "I free you now. I sorry this happen. Everyone mad Running Elk shot. They not know you good man like I do."

As much as Fargo wanted to go after the shooter, common sense dictated he must wait until daylight. He rubbed his wrists and said, "I'm still hungry. Any chance I can get some food?"

"I have woman bring," Small Badger said. He addressed his father and went to the flap. "I be back."

Gray Bear sat staring at the ground.

Fargo wondered what the chief was thinking about. He imagined that both father and son had gone against popular sentiment and stood up for him when the rest of the band wanted to hold him to account for the boy's death.

The silence was awkward. Off in the village a dog barked. Someone began playing a flute.

When the flap parted Fargo looked up, expecting it to be Small Badger. Instead, it was a warrior he had never seen before, a well-muscled man in his middle years. He came over to Gray Bear and the two had a brief exchange. The newcomer was angry. Twice he nodded at Fargo.

Small Badger returned. He seemed surprised that the other warrior was there. He listened to what the man had to say, and then turned. "This be Motomo, father to Running Elk. In the white tongue his name be He Who Goes First."

Fargo nodded.

Motomo glared.

Small Badger said something to him and that set off a long

argument. It ended when Motomo gestured at Fargo as if plunging a blade into his body.

Gray Bear spoke.

Motomo stared sullenly at Fargo with raw hate in his eyes.

"What is that all about?" Fargo asked.

"Him still think you kill his son. Him think you not come to buy Appaloosas. Him think you come to steal. When Running Elk try to stop you, you shoot him."

"Didn't you explain about the shooter in the trees?"

"We tell him. Father say about tracks. Motomo think maybe men in trees your friends. He want you dead. Father say no. Father say must catch men. Then Motomo know truth."

"That's fair, I suppose," Fargo said.

"At dawn warriors track men in trees," Small Badger said. "Father say Motomo go." Small Badger paused. "You as well."

"Thank him for me."

Small Badger did, then glanced at the glowering Motomo and turned back to Fargo. "You my friend so I warn you. Be careful. Keep eyes sharp. Keep ears sharp. Motomo want you dead. He want you dead so much, maybe he not care other man not your friend. Maybe he kill you just to kill you. Understand?"

"I savvy. And thanks."

"I know you not do bad thing like this. But others not know you same as me." Small Badger sighed and shook his head. "My English is much bad, yes?"

"You do fine for the short time the missionary was with your people, and how young you were," Fargo complimented him. He didn't mention how much better Many Clouds spoke it.

As if that were a stage cue, the flap parted and in came the lady herself. She carried a wooden bowl heaped with chunks of cooked deer meat and boiled roots.

She came around the three warriors and knelt and placed the bowl in front of Fargo.

"I'm obliged," Fargo said.

Many Clouds smiled and stayed on her knees, her head bowed.

Gray Bear rose. He addressed his son and Motomo and made for the flap.

With a last glare at Fargo, Motomo followed.

Small Badger stood. "You must stay in lodge tonight. Warriors watch that you not get away. I sorry but it for your good."

"What about my horse?"

"I take care of him. I feed. I water." Small Badger walked to the flap. "I go with you in morning. I try make sure Motomo not kill you. Sleep well, friend." The flap closed behind him.

Fargo sighed and picked up the bowl. He ate with his fingers. The meat was delicious, the roots tasted a lot like potatoes. After his fourth piece he asked, "Are you going to say anything or give me the silent treatment?"

"Silent treatment?" Many Clouds repeated, looking up. "That is new to me. What does it mean?"

"You're not going to talk because you're mad at me."

Many Clouds placed her hand on his knee. "Why would I be mad? You never said you would stay with me. You did not make a promise you could not keep. Some men do that. Some lie to trick a woman into spreading her legs."

"Men can be real bastards," Fargo said with a grin.

Many Clouds didn't smile. "Small Badger picked me to bring your food. He knows you and I are friends. Some of the others, though . . ."

She stopped.

"I don't want you in trouble on my account."

"You are the talk of the village. Running Elk was well liked. Why did the man in the trees do it?"

"He was after me, not the boy. Running Elk charged him. There was nothing I could do."

"Do you know who the man in the trees was?"

"I've seen him before," Fargo admitted.

"Why does he want you dead?"

"I wish I knew." The question had been burning at Fargo since the attack. "I aim to wring it out of him when I catch him."

"You might not have the chance. The other warriors want vengeance. Running Elk's father wants those to blame dead most of all."

"I gathered that." Fargo selected another piece of meat and put it in his mouth but the meal had lost its savor.

"My people are not of one mind. Half think you killed the boy or were a party to killing him. Half think you did not."

"I'll prove to them I didn't."

Many Clouds slid her hand from his knee to his thigh. "Gray Bear picked three warriors to go with you tomorrow besides his son and Motomo. I know who they are. Two think you are not involved but the other is a good friend of Motomo's. You must watch both of them."

Fargo put his hand on hers. "I appreciate the warning."

Many Clouds pulled her hand away. "I would do more for you if I could," she said quietly.

"You're welcome to stay the night," Fargo suggested.

"As much as I would like to it would not be wise. Those who believe you are the killer would not like it."

"I understand."

"I do not care what they think but I have my parents and my brother and sisters to think of."

"Do what's best for you."

Many Clouds rose and kissed him on the cheek. Cupping his chin, she said earnestly, "If I were you I would escape the first chance there is. Forget the men in the trees."

"I can't."

Many Clouds straightened. "There is one other thing. It is all over camp how you came to buy a stallion and a mare for a white man to breed. Is this true?"

Fargo nodded.

"Many do not like this. Some who think you did not kill

54

the boy are against you because of it. Your situation is . . ." Many Clouds stopped. "Complicated. Is that the right word?"

"It fits as good as anything."

Many Clouds went to the flap. "Do your best to stay alive. I hold you dear in my heart and it would make me sad if they kill you."

"That makes two of us," Skye Fargo said.

8

The day had dawned cloudy with the scent of rain in the air.

Dappled by shadows, the Nez Perce rode in single file. Their tracker was exceptionally good.

Fargo had offered to help but Motomo objected. He insisted that Fargo ride at the middle of the line with warriors in front of him and in back of him so he couldn't try to flee.

"I sorry," Small Badger said as they started out. "Him cause much trouble if we not do as he want."

Motomo and Motomo's friend were behind Fargo, arrows nocked to the strings of their bow. It made his skin prickle to think that they were looking for an excuse—any excuse—to sink a shaft into him.

Fargo wished he had the Colt and the Henry. His guns were back in the village in Gray Bear's lodge. He'd asked for them and Small Badger told him he would get them back after they found Running Elk's killer and Motomo was convinced he had no part in the killing.

Over the past hour the wind had picked up. Fargo reckoned the storm would break before the afternoon was out, and if the rain was heavy enough it would make tracking a lot harder, if not impossible.

Small Badger slowed and let the Ovaro come up next to him. "How you be, Iron Will?"

"How do you think?" Fargo wasn't in the best of moods. To be held a prisoner rankled, even if he did understand why they were doing it. What he didn't understand was the motive of the shooter. He needed to talk to him but the Nez Perce weren't likely to give him the chance.

"We find three men before sun go down," Small Badger predicted. "Then this be over."

"Has your pa made up his mind about parting with a couple of horses?" Fargo brought up.

"We talk last night. I say we should. Him worried whites let other tribes have m'a min to breed."

"What if the man who buys them gives his word he will only sell them to whites?"

"My father say him decide by time we back at village. He let you know then."

"Provided I make it back," Fargo amended.

Small Badger glanced over his shoulder at Motomo. "I do what I can to protect you."

The woodland became strangely still. Normally birds would be singing and squirrels would scamper along the high limbs and rabbits would bound off at their approach. But not a single creature was to be seen or heard.

The tracks showed that the shooter and his two friends had held to a gallop for almost two miles. Evidently they had expected the Nez Perce to come after them. When no pursuit developed they had slowed to a walk.

The tracker found where the three men had camped for the night. Mixed with the charred embers of the fire were a few rabbit bones. The warrior also discovered a clear track made by a moccasin.

"The three be Indians!" Small Badger exclaimed.

Not quite, Fargo thought.

Hour followed hour. The whole time, Fargo swore he could feel Motomo's eyes bore into his back. He hid his unease and was glad he still had the toothpick in his boot.

Along about the middle of the afternoon the clouds darkened and the wind rose to a shriek. The Nez Perce were pushing hard to overtake the killers but they still hadn't caught sight of them when thunder rumbled in the distance.

Fargo noticed that Motomo and Motomo's friend were riding side by side and talking in low tones. The looks they gave him would wither a cactus.

"It rain heavy soon," Small Badger stated the obvious.

A flash split the sky far off. More thunder pealed, and the wind howled. Saplings bent and limbs thrashed.

The warrior who was tracking drew rein. Sliding down, he sank to one knee and studied the ground. He said something.

"The three men ride fast again," Small Badger translated.

"Maybe they know we're after them," Fargo speculated. "We should pick up the pace or we won't catch them before the storm strikes."

The thunder grew louder, the wind was a constant banshee wail. A tree limb broke with a loud *snap* and went flying off. The brush rustled and crackled and popped.

"We get wet soon," Small Badger said.

They pressed on over a sawtooth ridge and down a slope of heavy timber. The warrior in the lead abruptly drew rein and hollered.

Fargo saw it, too—tendrils of smoke rising above a stand of cottonwoods on the other side of a valley.

"We find killer!" Small Badger cried, elated.

Eager to get down there, Fargo gigged the Ovaro. He went only a few yards when Motomo came up on his right and Motomo's friend on his left. The friend thrust the tip of a lance within inches of his chest and Motomo motioned for him to stop.

"What the hell?"

Small Badger reined in next to the Ovaro and swapped a curt flurry with Motomo. "He think you go warn your friends. He say you to stay with us."

"They're not my damn friends."

"Better you let us go," Small Badger advised. "Better you stay back with Alahmoot." He bobbed his chin at Motomo's friend.

Against his better judgment Fargo relented. Small Badger and Motomo and the other two warriors started down the mountain. He followed, conscious that Alahmoot was ready to hurl a lance if he made any sudden movements.

The first raindrops fell, large and cold, spattering Fargo on the cheek and the neck.

To the west a lightning bolt cleaved the heavens and a thunderclap rumbled, its echo rolling on and on.

It took five minutes to descend and by then the drops were a drizzle. Fargo drew rein at the tree line. The Nez Perce were circling around rather than cutting across in the open.

Fargo leaned on his saddle horn, and fumed. He should be with them. Too much could go wrong. The Nez Perce had bows and lances. Their quarry was armed with rifles and pistols. He looked at Alahmoot and said, "We should help them."

The warrior was a statue.

Fargo resorted to sign language. The sign for "help" was a combination of the signs for "work" and "with." "We must work with them."

Alahmoot didn't respond or speak.

Off across the valley the Nez Perce were closing in on the cottonwoods. Small Badger was in the lead. They dismounted and left their horses tied to trees and closed in on foot.

Fargo could barely make them out for the drizzle. Call it intuition, call it a hunch, but he suddenly had a gut feeling that the Nez Perce were blundering into an ambush. The cottonwoods were too quiet, almost as if the smoke had been a ruse to draw them in. "God, no," he said. Should anything happen to Small Badger, Motomo and Alahmoot wouldn't hesitate to try to kill him.

Figures moved in the cottonwoods.

Fargo opened his mouth to shout a warning but it was too late. Rifles cracked, spitting lead and smoke. One of the Nez Perce dropped. War whoops rose and Fargo thought he saw arrows cleave the air. Hooves pounded and three riders burst from the far end of the cottonwoods and raced on up the valley. The killer and his friends were fleeing. It could be, Fargo guessed, that they weren't sure exactly how many Nez Perce they were up against and decided to get gone while they could.

The loudest thunderclap yet signaled Nature's full tantrum. The storm erupted in all its elemental fury. The rain fell in torrents, a deluge so heavy, Fargo couldn't see his hand at arm's length.

It was the moment Fargo had been waiting for. Instantly, he reined away from Alahmoot and made off through the woods in the direction the three riders had gone. He wasn't worried about Alahmoot hearing him above the din of the storm, so he brought the Ovaro to a gallop.

Some would call it reckless. All Fargo had was the tooth-pick, and here he was chasing three men who were well armed.

From well behind him came a shout of alarm. Alahmoot had discovered he was gone.

Fargo grimly smiled. He intended to find out what the hell was going on, provided the storm didn't spoil everything. He had gone but a short way when he was soaked to the skin. The rain was a sheet of pebbles, battering him relentlessly. The smart thing was to find cover, but how, when he couldn't see? To make it worse, he had to haul on the reins and take it slow or risk colliding with a tree.

Long minutes of wet and cold ensued. By Fargo's best reckoning he was near the end of the valley when a dark shape hove out of the downpour. It was a bluff, the sides sheer and high. He rode up to it, and, sheltered from the worst of the tempest, gratefully drew rein.

Fargo placed his hand on his empty holster and frowned. No matter what happened he must return to the Nez Perce village for his weapons. He supposed he could always buy a new Colt and a new Henry but he was used to the ones he had and reluctant to part with them.

The storm proved to be a monster. It pummeled the earth for more than an hour. Then, abruptly, it ended. The rain ceased and the dark clouds floated off and dazzling sunlight splashed the drenched vegetation.

Fargo gigged the Ovaro. He doubted he would find tracks. The rain had seen to that. But he was fairly sure the three would continue to the southeast so it was to the southeast he reined the stallion.

He hoped to overtake them by sunset but it wasn't to be. The golden orb was roosting on the rim of creation when he drew rein in a gully with high walls. Climbing down, he gathered wood for a fire. It took forever to find enough dry branches. Once flames were crackling, he put coffee on, then stripped down to his bare skin, spread out his wet buckskins and his socks, and sat close to the fire until he was dry. In his saddlebags were a spare set of buckskins and socks. The shirt was torn and the socks had holes but he put them on anyway.

Fargo felt warm again. He felt even better after a cup of piping-hot coffee.

His stomach growled, so he helped himself to pemmican.

The night was alive with howls and shrieks and roars but none of the meat-eaters came near. Normally he would sit up until near midnight but he turned in early in order to head out early. His sleep was undisturbed. An hour before sunrise his inner clock woke him. He was up and in the saddle as the sky to the east brightened.

Fargo brought the stallion to a trot. There was a good chance the three hadn't broken camp yet. He constantly sniffed the air and soon was rewarded with the scent of wood smoke. Ahead, the slopes of two mountains converged, blocking his view. He rode through the gap and beheld a wooded strip—and an orange glimmer off through the pines.

Fargo reined up. He tied the stallion, patted it, and crept toward the fire.

From trunk to trunk and bush to bush he worked his way closer until he was within a stone's throw of a clearing. Crouching, he took in every little detail.

Two of the three half-breeds were still asleep. Only the one with the bushy eyebrows, Speckled Wolf, was up. He was cutting strips of squirrel meat and skewering them.

Fargo slid his hand under his pant leg and into his boot. Palming the Arkansas toothpick, he stealthily glided nearer. He wouldn't kill them until he had some answers.

Speckled Wolf stretched and yawned and scratched himself. His Sharps was next to him. His revolver, a Volcanic, was tucked under his belt. He also had an antler-handled knife on his hip.

The trick was for Fargo to get close without being shot. Flattening, he crawled, his chin brushing the ground. He came to a log, took off his hat, and carefully peered over.

Speckled Wolf had stopped slicing squirrel. He glanced to the east and said gruffly, "Get up, you two. The sun will be up soon."

Neither stirred.

Scowling, Speckled Wolf went over and kicked each of them in turn.

"I won't tell you again. I want to be in the saddle at daybreak."

The other two half-breeds sat up. One rubbed his leg where Speckled Wolf had kicked him.

"What the hell is the hurry? They'll never catch us. That storm wiped out our tracks."

"Maybe it did and maybe it didn't. Either way, I won't rest easy until we're shed of their territory."

"You spook too easy these days."

"Go to hell, Rooster," Speckled Wolf said.

The third breed said, "I don't blame you for wanting to get the hell out of here. The Nez Perce will be out for your hide after you went and shot that kid."

"I told you, Ferret Killer. I had no choice. He saw me. He came at me with an arrow ready to fly."

"I know. I was just saying, was all."

"What about Fargo?" Rooster asked.

"Nothing has changed. We still have to stop him. I tried the easy way by taking his horse but he caught us. I tried to wing him at the Nez Perce village and missed. So now we do it the hard way."

Rooster said a strange thing. "I sort of feel bad about it. It's not his fault. He wasn't there. He doesn't know what we know."

"Doesn't matter," Speckled Wolf replied.

"Say it plain," Ferret Killer said.

"Do I have to? You both know what's at stake. If we can't stop him then Fargo has to die."

9

To say Fargo was puzzled was an understatement. He'd taken it for granted Speckled Wolf tried to kill him. Now he learned the three breeds were trying to scare him off. But why? He needed to hear more.

Rooster and Ferret Killer got up and moved to the fire. They both could use a wash and their clothes had never seen suds. Ferret Killer slipped a hand under a ragged leather vest and produced a silver flask. Opening it, he sucked down a swallow and let out a contented sigh.

"The sun ain't even up," Speckled Wolf said.

"Don't start."

"I keep telling you but you won't listen. You're drinking yourself into an early grave."

"It's my life," Ferret Killer said sullenly. "Such as it is."

Rooster swore. "Don't you dare start in on how sorry you feel for yourself. I am so sick to death of your blabber I could shoot you."

"Stop right there," Speckled Wolf broke in. "I won't put up with it today. We are going to eat and saddle our horses and get the hell out of here, and we're going to do it without arguing."

"You're awful testy," Rooster said.

"I shot a kid two days ago. It's not something I'm proud of."

Ferret Killer tilted the flask to his lips. "It wouldn't bother me none. He tried to stick an arrow in you, didn't he? He had it coming."

"No, he didn't," Speckled Wolf said bitterly. "He was just doing what he was supposed to. I should have shot to wound him but it happened too damn fast."

Ferret Killer snickered. "Keep it up and Rooster will say you're feeling sorry for yourself like he always does me."

"Your problem is that you wish you weren't born a breed," Rooster said. "You wish you were born all white or all red."

"And you don't?" Ferret Killer rejoined.

Speckled Wolf angrily gestured. "Enough, damn it. If all you're going to do is bicker, keep your damn mouths shut."

Fargo put his hat back on and left the sanctuary of the log. He planned to sneak around to the other side of the clearing and jump them as they were heading out. If he could catch them off guard he might get his hands on one of their rifles or revolvers.

"It sure is funny, us going to all this bother," Ferret Killer said. "You'd think we had a stake in it."

"We do," Speckled Wolf said.

"Hell. None of us have any Nez Perce blood. You and me are part Crow and Rooster, here, is part Arapaho. We don't owe the Nez Perce."

"We owe it to all Indians."

Ferret Killer rolled his eyes. "There you go again, on your high horse. But I've got news for you. My red half doesn't mean as much to me as your red half means to you. Let them do it if they're dumb enough. It would serve them right."

Fargo was trying to make sense of what he was hearing. It almost sounded as if they thought they were doing the Nez Perce some kind of favor. He skirted a patch of high grass that might sway and give him away.

From out of the forest to the northwest came a loud whinny.

The three breeds leaped to their feet and brandished weapons.

"Did you hear that?" Ferret Killer exclaimed.

"We're not deaf," Speckled Wolf said. "Quick. Throw your saddles on. It must be the Nez Perce."

To Fargo it had sounded like the Ovaro. He crawled behind an oak and rose into a crouch and ran back the way he had come. The stallion wouldn't whinny like that unless something was wrong. It could be a grizzly or a mountain lion or maybe hungry wolves. He flew, fearing the worst and wishing yet again that he had his guns. He saw the Ovaro with its head high and its ear pricked and he burst out of the trees and looked in the direction it was looking.

From behind him came the drum of footsteps.

Fargo tried to spin but strong arms encircled his chest and other arms wrapped around his legs and he was borne to the ground with a bone-jolting crash. He still had the toothpick in his hand and fell on top of it. Fortunately, the blade didn't stick him. He slid the knife up his sleeve just as he was roughly rolled onto his back and a moccasin was pressed to his chest.

The moccasin belonged to Motomo. It was Alahmoot who had him around the legs. Another warrior stood a few feet away with an arrow notched.

"Fancy running into you," Fargo said.

Small Badger came up. "I be sorry, friend. I not want to come after you but Motomo not let you get away. Him want your blood for son."

Fargo was jerked to his feet and shoved toward the Ovaro. Motomo motioned for him to climb on. The warrior with the bow kept the arrow trained on him, and Motomo took the reins and started into the forest to the northwest. Small Badger walked alongside.

"We ride all night to find you. Hunt and hunt and finally find tracks of horse."

Fargo glanced back. He couldn't see the campfire; Speckled Wolf and his friends had put it out. The Nez Perce could catch them if he said something. He didn't. He couldn't exactly say why but he held his tongue.

"Why you run?" Small Badger asked.

"You would have done the same in my boots."

"That no answer. I trust you. I tell others you not have

part in killing Running Elk. Now them not believe me. They say if you not do it, why you try get away."

Fargo didn't answer.

Their horses weren't far. Motomo and Alahmoot rode behind Fargo; Small Badger and the other warrior in front. Motomo made a comment that caused Alahmoot to smile and Small Badger to frown.

"Him say he hope you try to get away again so he can kill you like you kill his son."

On the entire ride to the village they watched Fargo like hawks watching prey. Even so, he managed to slip the toothpick into his boot. When they made camp that night they bound him. He could have cut himself free but he elected to go along with them for the time being.

The dead warrior was belly down on his horse. His name meant Fierce In A Fight and he had been the first to rush the stand of cottonwoods and had been shot down before he could reach them.

Fargo asked if the Nez Perce had gotten a good look at the shooters and Small Badger replied that they had not thanks to the rain, although, "I see face of one and he look like Crow."

Along about the middle of the afternoon they reached the village. Once again everyone came out to meet them. Fargo was hauled from the Ovaro and taken to the same lodge as before. Motomo shoved him through the flap so hard, Fargo fell to his knees. His temper flared but he reminded himself the man had lost a son.

He lay on his side near the charred remains of the fire and mulled over what he should do. As much as he liked the Nez Perce, and as much as he needed the money Clarence Bell was willing to pay him, he was tempting fate if he stayed.

The sky darkened. The village grew quiet. It was the supper hour and most of the Nez Perce were in their lodges.

Fargo rolled onto his back. He had to strain to reach his boots. He slipped his fingers in and pried at the toothpick but it was stuck in the sheath. He was so intent on getting it that he almost missed the swish of the flap. Quickly, he pulled his hand from his boot and looked to see who it was. "So much for that bear being an omen."

Many Clouds was carrying a bowl of food. "I cannot help it you keep coming back and I cannot stay away." She set down the bowl. "I brought elk meat with wild onions and carrots."

Fargo sat up. They had not fed him much on the trail and he was famished. "What's the latest about me?"

"Gray Bear and the elders are in council. They will decide your fate. Motomo has spoken to them and demanded a life for a life. Small Badger has asked them to spare you."

"I'm back where I started." Fargo opened his mouth and she popped a thick piece of meat in. He chewed lustily, then said, "I suppose I can forget about buying horses."

"That, too, is in the hands of the council. It could be to-night, it could be tomorrow." Many Clouds glanced at the flap and lowered her voice. "I do not want you to die."

"Makes two of us."

"I am serious." Many Clouds fed him a carrot. "I will come back later after everyone is asleep and cut you loose. You must take your horse and go."

"What about my guns?"

"Gray Bear has them. To try and take them from his lodge would only get you caught."

Fargo held out his wrists. "Why wait? Cut the rope now."

"No. I know you. You will try for your guns and be killed. Now be quiet while I feed you."

Fargo was too hungry to argue.

Many Clouds had more to say. "You do not seem to understand. I take a great risk helping you. My people would not harm me if they found out but they would not be pleased with me, either."

"I wouldn't do anything to get you in trouble."

"So you say. But what if a warrior tries to stop you?" Many Clouds held an onion to his mouth. "I do not want any of my tribe hurt." She touched his chin and ran the tip of her finger over his beard to his throat. "I like your hair. Our men are always smooth."

"You have smooth parts I like," Fargo told her. She went on feeding him and he went on eating. When she caressed his arm from his shoulder to his elbow he didn't think much of it. When she dallied her hand from his knee to his hip he figured she was being affectionate. But after he ate the last morsel and she leaned forward and kissed him full on the mouth hard and longingly, he awoke to what she was up to. "You can't be thinking what I think you're thinking."

Many Clouds set down the bowl and placed both her hands on his thighs. "Why not?"

"What if someone comes in?"

"No one will come until the council has decided. No one wants anything to do with you."

"They'll wonder why you're in here so long."

"They know I am your friend." Many Clouds kissed him on the neck and on the cheek, her lips soft and warm.

"I can't do it with my hands tied."

"Listen to you," Many Clouds teased. "I never thought there would come a time when *you* would not want to."

"Don't put words in my mouth," Fargo huffed. Of course he wanted to, just not then and there.

"I would rather put something else." Many Clouds kissed him and this time her silken tongue met his.

Despite himself, Fargo grew aroused. "The rope, damn it," he said when she drew back.

"No."

"I can't touch you."

"That is all right. I can touch you."

"You little minx. You aim to have your way with me whether I take part or not."

"The idea appeals to me, yes." Many Clouds rose and went to the flap and tied it. As she came back she hiked at her dress and when she reached him she was naked save for her moccasins. "Do you like what you see?"

"Was that a trick question?" Fargo was mesmerized by her full breasts and jutting nipples and the dark triangle at the junction of her thighs. His mouth watered as if he were starved for the food he just ate.

Grinning impishly, Many Clouds stopped, her navel inches from his face. "Can you tell how much I want you?"

Fargo sniffed and kissed her navel and her skin fluttered. "Yes," he said, the simple word sounding strained.

"If you really want me to leave"—Many Clouds rubbed her bush against his chin—"say so."

Fargo could barely talk for the constriction in his throat. He was hot all over and hardening where it counted. "I'd spank your backside if my hands were free."

"I might like that." Sinking to her knees, Many Clouds cupped a breast and offered it to him. "Only if you want," she baited him.

A low growl issued from Fargo's throat. Lowering his head, he sucked the nipple into his mouth and tweaked it with the tips of his teeth. She moaned and dug her nails into his arm.

"I must be crazy to do this but you make me feel so good. While you were gone, all I could think of was this."

Fargo nipped harder. He lathered her breast and switched to the other and did the same. Her bosom began to rise and fall and her breathing became husky with desire.

"I like this very much," Many Clouds said softly. "I can have my way with you and there is nothing you can do."

"Think so, do you?" Fargo bent even lower and nuzzled her thatch. She gasped and recoiled but then ground against his face, her own reddening with raw lust.

Many Clouds entwined her fingers in his hair and pulled him closer. "How do you do this to me?"

Fargo couldn't say. His mouth was occupied. He darted his tongue out and in and felt her stiffen. He thought it was because of him until she put her hands on his shoulders and pushed him away. Confused, he raised his head.

Many Clouds pointed.

Someone was hitting the flap.

10

A male voice called out.

Many Clouds stepped back and took a moment to compose herself before she responded in a calm, level tone.

Fargo got the gist of it. The warrior standing guard wanted to know why the flap was tied. She told the warrior that she was feeding him, that his hands were bound and he couldn't do it himself. Since it was the custom among the Nez Perce to close the flap when the occupants did not wish to be disturbed, she allayed the warrior's suspicions. He told her not to keep it tied too long.

Many Clouds motioned to Fargo to be silent and crept to the flap. She pressed an ear to it and listened a bit, then came back and whispered, "It is all right. If we are quiet he will not suspect."

"You must really want me," Fargo teased.

Many Clouds colored and smiled. "You are like honey. A sweetness I cannot get enough of."

"Make it easy." Fargo shifted and pumped his wrists. "Untie me," he tried again.

Many Clouds came up to him and placed her flat belly against his face. "Do your best as you are."

Fargo bit her but not too hard. She squeaked and grinned and then put her hands on either side of his head and rubbed her belly back and forth. He rimmed her navel with his tongue, and then licked lower, down her right thigh and up her left. Her skin was as soft as silk, her scent intoxicating. He nuzzled her and she gasped and then she slowly eased onto her back and wantonly parted her legs.

"I should stop," Fargo said. "It would serve you right."

"You won't."

"You think you have me figured out."

Many Clouds cupped her breasts and pinched her nipples and parted her mouth in a delectable O. "When it comes to this, yes. You like it more than you like anything."

"I won't forget what you've done."

"It would please me to be remembered."

Fargo balanced on his knees, and bent. He licked and delved, the while she squirmed and cooed and mashed against him ever harder as her need climbed. When she could not take it any longer she sat up and pulled his pants down around his knees. She bid him sit and straddled him. Then, smiling like a cat about to devour a canary, she gripped his member and stroked.

The sensation almost made Fargo explode. All he could do was sit there, teetering on the brink, until she rose up and slowly impaled herself.

"God," Fargo said.

Many Clouds pumped up and down in a rising tempo of unbridled passion.

He tried to inhale a nipple but she was moving so fast her breasts jiggled wildly. Throwing back her head, she arched her body in a bow, her nails raking his shoulders.

"Yes. Oh yes."

Fargo listened for the guard. She was slapping against him loud enough to be heard but she didn't care. She was at the apex and about to plunge into the abyss of release. Her nails dug deeper, so deep it hurt. To get back at her he bit her shoulder.

Many Clouds stiffened and her eyes grew wide. Stifling an outcry, she went over the brink. She gushed and gushed.

Fargo let himself go. He rammed up into her as best he could sitting on the ground, using the balls of his feet for extra leverage. Again and again he drove up and in until he was drained and spent.

Many Clouds sagged against his chest and pecked him on the left cheek and then the right. "That was nice."

"Glad you had a good time."

"You liked it too." Grinning, she reached down and patted his manhood. "The woman who can have this every night will live her life happy."

"Was that a hint?"

She chuckled, and grabbed her dress. "I will bring you more food if you are still hungry."

Fargo nodded at his groin. "Aren't you forgetting something?"

"I thought I would leave you like that." Many Clouds laughed and squatted and pulled his clothes together. "There. Now you are presentable. Is that the right word?"

"It works both ways," Fargo said.

"What does?"

"The man who gets to have you every night will be a lucky gent. You're more playful than most."

Many Clouds tenderly touched his lips and trembled slightly. "That was a kind thing to say. You act mean at times yet you have a nice heart."

"Like hell I do."

"You need not be ashamed. Among my people, for a warrior to be a leader he must not only be brave and wise, he must have a good heart."

Fargo was aware that other tribes also valued kindness and compassion as much as courage. "So I've heard."

"Gray Bear has a good heart. He always advises what is best for everyone, even our enemies." Many Clouds kissed him and skipped to the flap. She untied it, then pursed her lips and blew him a kiss. "I will hope for the best for you." Ducking her head, she went out.

Fargo settled back. All he could do was wait. He closed his eyes and figured to drift off but he hadn't been lying there long when the flap rustled and in came their leader with his son in tow. Fargo sat up and tried to read his fate in their faces.

Father and son sat with their legs crossed and Small Badger began by announcing, "Our council did decide."

"I get to live?"

Small Badger looked at Gray Bear, who went on at some length. "My t'o t, sorry, my father, speak for you with council. Him say you good friend to Nimipuu. Him say you always talk straight tongue."

"Thank him for me," Fargo interrupted.

Small Badger did, and then continued. "Him say he believe you not kill Running Elk. Him say it be three men warriors find. He think they try steal m'a min. Him say you should live."

"And?" Fargo prompted when the younger warrior stopped.

"Motomo argue. Him say you bad man. Him say you kill son. He want you dead. Only few take his side. Most believe my father. It decided you not enemy. It decided you our friend." Smiling, Small Badger produced his knife and moved around behind Fargo and cut him free.

"I'm obliged." Rubbing his wrists, Fargo asked the question uppermost on his mind. "But when do I get my guns back?"

"I bring soon. First Father want know more about white man who want our horses."

Fargo told them everything he knew about Clarence Bell and the Circle B and Bell's offer. "I have a thousand dollars in my saddlebags and the rest is yours when I bring him the Appaloosas."

Gray Bear asked if it was true that five thousand was a lot of money. Fargo said it was, even for a white man, and that in his opinion the rancher was being generous. Gray Bear remarked that he could do a lot of good for his people. He then asked if Fargo trusted Bell.

Fargo chose his words with care. "He seems honest enough. But I hardly know the man."

"We get rest of money when him get horses, is that right?" Small Badger asked.

Fargo confirmed that was how whites often conducted business.

The chief and his son conversed. Finally Small Badger turned to Fargo and said, "Father say we sell you m'a min. One stallion, one mare. In morning we go look at herd and you pick."

"I already have," Fargo said. "I've seen a mare I like and I'll show her to you. The stallion I'd like to buy is Thunderhoof."

The young warrior gave a start. "Him Father's horse."

"I know."

"Him father's *best* horse."

"For five thousand dollars Bell should get the best."

Another long talk took place. Fargo could tell that Gray Bear wasn't entirely happy with his choice.

"Father must think on this," Small Badger related. "Him give you decision in morning."

They rose to go.

"My guns," Fargo reminded the youth.

"In morning."

Fargo hid his disappointment. The important thing was that he was on friendly terms again. He walked with them to the flap and then tied it and laid down to rest. He only intended to take a short nap but when he opened his eyes the lodge was plunged in gloom and the opening at the top was dark. He had slept much too long. He blamed Many Clouds.

About to sit up, Fargo stiffened. He was sure he had heard someone move.

Pretending to still be asleep, he rolled onto his side and mumbled, as sleepers sometimes did, and cracked his eyelids. The flap was still closed and he saw no one else. He figured to get a fire going and was set to rise when a gust of wind moved the flap and moonlight spilled in.

A patch of shadow darker than the rest became the darkling form of a man in a crouch. Fargo figured it must be Motomo, come to avenge his son. He raised his pant leg high enough to palm the Arkansas toothpick.

Fargo stayed on his side. He would let Motomo come to him. He held the toothpick behind his knee and marked the distance and when only a few feet separated them, he sprang up. "That's close enough."

The warrior spat words in Nez Perce and attacked.

A knife arced at Fargo's neck. He countered with the toothpick. Steel rang on steel and they circled. Only then did Fargo see who it was. He had been wrong. It wasn't Motomo. It was Alahmoot. "I didn't kill the boy, damn you."

Alahmoot swept in quick and low, thrusting at Fargo's groin. Fargo sidestepped. He stabbed at Fargo's ribs. Fargo dodged. He swung again and the blade clipped a whang on Fargo's buckskins.

They resumed circling.

Fargo was averse to killing him. He had just gone through hell to get the Nez Perce to sell him a couple of horses. Killing a warrior now might ruin any hope he had. Accordingly, when Alahmoot lunged, seeking to disembowel him, Fargo twisted aside and slashed.

Alahmoot hissed and leaped back, blood misting from his forearm. He pressed it against his side to stanch the spray and came in again.

Fargo avoided a stab at his throat and another at his stomach. Pivoting, he streaked the toothpick and opened the warrior's thigh. More blood spurted.

Alahmoot grimaced in pain and tottered.

Fargo hoped that would do it. He motioned at the flap and said, "Get the hell out while you can." He knew the warrior didn't speak English but his meaning was clear.

Alahmoot's shirtsleeve dripped blood and a dark stain was spreading down his leg but he bared his teeth and lanced his blade at Fargo's neck. Once again steel met steel. Fargo, tucking down and under, cut Alahmoot's other leg, and cut it deep.

The warrior staggered. He lowered his knife and looked down at himself.

"Give up, damn you."

Hatred twisted Alahmoot's features. He said something under his breath and turned and limped to the flap. He looked back at Fargo and motioned with his knife across his throat. The meaning was clear. It wasn't over. Alahmoot would kill him yet. The warrior slipped out, leaving a dark smear.

Fargo wiped the toothpick clean on his pants. Holding on to it, he went to the entrance and warily peered out. A warrior stood a few yards away, his back to the lodge. Either Alahmoot had snuck past him or the warrior had let Alahmoot slip inside knowing full well what he intended.

Fargo found where the ties had been cut. He retied them and set about rekindling the fire. A stack of wood against the far side ensured he wouldn't want for fuel. Soon crackling flames were spreading warmth. He sat facing the entrance, the toothpick in his hand, until the flap bulged and Many Clouds called out.

"Let me in."

Fargo admitted her. This time she had brought roast elk and potatoes and a biscuit made from flour and berries. "Are you trying to fatten me up so I'll take to lodge life?" he joked.

"There is an idea."

After their lovemaking and his fight with Alahmoot, Fargo was hungry again. He dug in with relish.

Many Clouds sat. She put her hand on the ground and then raised it and stared at her palm. "This is blood."

Fargo chewed lustily.

"Fresh blood."

"I had a visitor." Fargo elaborated, and when he was done she angrily rose to her feet.

"I will go talk to Gray Bear. He will not be happy. The council decided you were to be spared."

"I'd be obliged if you didn't," Fargo said.

"But Alahmoot tried to *kill* you. He will try again, or Motomo will. My people must know so they can be stopped."

"No. It will only make Motomo madder. I'll deal with him in my own way and my own time."

"I do not understand," Many Clouds confessed. "I offer you our protection. Refuse, and you might not make it out of these mountains alive."

Fargo chuckled and bit into a piece of juicy elk meat and said with his mouth full. "What else is new?"

11

Some whites liked to say that Indians didn't know the value of a dollar. They joked that Indians traded prime pelts for pennies or gave up thousands of square miles of land for a few trinkets and blankets. They overlooked the fact that the Indians were often tricked, and that the Indian concept of land was not the same as the white man's.

But early on, the Indians learned how dearly the white man dearly loved his money. They learned that with it they could obtain guns and steel knives and pots and pans and all the wonderful things the white man possessed that they didn't.

Gray Bear was no fool. He understood that five thousand dollars was a considerable sum and could benefit his people greatly. It was the reason he gave for showing up at the lodge at first light with the stallion Thunderhoof and an exceptional mare. He also brought the Ovaro.

Fargo couldn't be happier, especially after Small Badger gave him the Colt and the Henry. He checked that both were loaded and twirled the Colt into his holster. He shoved the Henry in the saddle scabbard. From his saddlebags he took the thousand dollars and gave it to Gray Bear.

"I'll do my best to get those horses to Clarence Bell safely," Fargo pledged.

Small Badger, who was translating, smiled. "We get them safe together. Father want me take two warriors go with you."

"I can do it on my own," Fargo objected. He was thinking of Speckled Wolf's bunch.

Gray Bear replied through his son. "You want m'a min, we go too. We help protect horses. We bring back rest of money from rancher."

That stopped Fargo in his mental tracks. He had no hankering to ride all the way back with the payment. "Who are the other warriors?"

"Motomo is one."

"Are you loco?"

"The other be a warrior called Kicking Bird. Alahmoot want come but him hurt legs somehow."

"Why in hell take Motomo? The man wants me dead."

"It only way council agree. Motomo not trust you. He go so be sure you not cheat Nimipuu."

"You know I wouldn't do that."

"I know and Father know but others not so sure. This way all of us are happy."

Except Fargo. It was bad enough he'd have to watch out for the breeds. Now he'd need eyes in the back of his head to keep Motomo from sticking a knife between his shoulder blades. "I don't like it. Not one bit."

"You want Appaloosas, they must go," Gray Bear insisted through Small Badger.

Fargo saw no way out short of returning to Bell empty-handed. "I reckon you leave me no choice."

"I sorry, friend."

Gray Bear had been looking at the ground and at the flap. "There be blood all over," his son translated.

Fargo made a show of acting surprised. "So there is."

"Blood not here last night."

"I didn't notice."

"Father want know if Alahmoot pay you visit?"

"I didn't notice," Fargo said again.

They were to leave when the sun was a hand's width above the horizon. Small Badger and his father excused themselves so Small Badger could get ready.

Fargo made coffee. He was expecting a visitor, and sure

enough, Many Clouds showed up wearing a doeskin dress that molded to her enticingly. He offered her coffee but she politely refused, and held out her hand.

"I only came to say how good it was to see you again. I will miss you." She lowered her voice. "I also came to warn you not to trust Motomo."

"As if I would."

"There is much whispering in the village," Many Clouds said ominously. "The whispers say you will not live to reach the rancher."

Fargo thanked her for the warning. She embraced him, and her lips brushed his neck.

"If you are ever again near Nimipuu land, come see me."

"You can count on it."

Bowing her head, Many Clouds hurried out.

Fargo was in the saddle, holding the lead rope to the Appaloosas, when Small Badger and the other two warriors rode up. Small Badger was smiling and eager for adventure. Motomo glowered. Kicking Bird was introduced and gave no clue to his feelings.

The village turned out to see them depart. Many patted Thunderhoof and the mare, acting as if they were saying good-bye to dear friends.

At last, to Fargo's relief, Small Badger gave the word and they headed out. The chief's son took the lead.

Fargo looked back only once. All the Nez Perce had gone on about their daily routines except for Gray Bear, who stood watching them until he was a speck in the distance.

At midday they rested. Again, about three. Not once did Thunderhoof or the mare give Fargo trouble.

That night they camped on a shelf flanked by spruce. Kicking Bird got the fire going. Motomo sat apart, and glared.

"He's not fixing to do that the whole way, is he?" Fargo said to Small Badger. "A man could get tired of it real quick."

The young warrior addressed Motomo, whose angry retort brought a flush of red.

"What did he say?"

"I have no right tell him how to look at you. Him say you have bad heart. Him say he watch you day and night."

It was going to be a long ride, Fargo reflected. Still, he had Thunderhoof and the mare, and in two weeks or less his job would be done and he could light a shuck for Denver and treat himself to women, whiskey and cards. Life didn't get any better than that.

About ten they were ready to turn in. Motomo argued that Fargo shouldn't help stand watch because he couldn't be trusted. Small Badger said that he trusted Fargo as much as he did his own father. Kicking Bird put an end to the dispute by saying that they would get more rest if all four of them took turns.

It seemed to Fargo that his head barely touched the ground than he was awakened. The night was peaceful, and he sat at the fire sipping coffee until his turn was over.

Motomo was to stand watch next. Fargo went over to wake him, and stopped short. Motomo was lying on his belly with his arm under him. Motomo's knife sheath, Fargo noticed, was empty. Instead of bending down and shaking him, Fargo poked Motomo's leg with a boot. He had to do it three times before Motomo rolled over. In Motomo's right hand was the knife.

"Fixing to stab me by mistake, were you?" Fargo said, and went to his blankets.

It proved hard to get back to sleep. Fargo could feel Motomo's eyes on him.

Eventually he dozed off but his rest was fitful.

A pink band heralded the new dawn.

Small Badger had been unusually quiet the previous day and started off the morning by hardly saying three words. Fargo was curious why and came right out and asked him as they got under way.

"I worry a lot," the young warrior confessed. "I worry Motomo try kill you. I worry you kill Motomo. I worry something happen to Thunderhoof or mare. I worry I not get back to village with money."

"That's a heap of worrying," Fargo agreed with a grin.

"It not funny. Father give big . . ." Small Badger paused. "What be that white word? I remember. Father give me big responsibility. I must not let Father down."

"You'll do fine," Fargo sought to reassure him. "You have the makings of a fine warrior."

"You mean that?"

"I don't say a thing just to flap my gums."

"That true. You say what you mean and mean what you say." Small Badger smiled. "You best white I know. You much like Nimipuu in how you think."

"In a few ways, maybe."

"In here." Small Badger touched his chest. "And it here that count."

The sun shone and the birds sang and by the middle of the morning Small Badger had relaxed enough to gab up a storm about everything from the best time of the year to hunt mountain sheep to the best way to cure a buffalo hide. Fargo was almost sorry he got him to loosen up.

They stopped to rest their mounts. Small Badger came over to pat Thunderhoof and admitted, "I will miss him very much. I thought maybe one day Father give him to me."

"You should have said something sooner," Fargo said. He might have asked for a different stallion.

Small Badger affectionately ran his hand over Thunderhoof's neck. "As you say, five thousand lot of money. Father say we go trading post. Every warrior have new rifle, every woman have whatever she want."

"Money does have its uses." Fargo thought of a certain fallen angel, and chuckled. She charged more than most but a night with her was worth every cent and then some.

"I not realize," Small Badger said. "Money always seem strange to me. Now I see why whites like it."

"Whites couldn't get by without it. For some, it's all they think of."

"Those who like be rich, yes?" Small Badger gazed over the stallion at him. "How come you never want be rich?"

Fargo motioned at the vista of virgin forest and towering peaks. "These are my riches."

"Sorry?"

"I like the wilds more than I do a big mansion or fine food or a fancy carriage."

"Like I say, you much like us." Small Badger looked past Fargo and his eyes narrowed. "What you want?" he asked in English, forgetting himself. Then he posed the question in his own tongue.

Motomo walked up and patted Thunderhoof. He answered, sneering at Fargo as he did.

"Him say him not agree with father about selling horse," Small Badger translated. "Him say if up to him, you not leave village alive."

"Tell him the only reason he's not dead is his son."

Both Small Badger and Motomo were puzzled by the remark.

"How that be? Him and I not savvy."

"I liked Running Elk. He was a good kid and treated me decent. He didn't deserve to die like that. It was partly my fault."

Small Badger was startled. He translated, and Motomo appeared surprised.

"How you mean it your fault?"

To suit his own purpose, Fargo had decided to tell them everything. "Those men you saw in the cottonwoods. I ran into them a while back. They tried to steal my horse. I made the mistake of letting them live but didn't reckon on ever seeing them again. Then they showed up out of the blue near your village that day and took a shot at me. Running Elk thought they were after your herd and tried to stop them and they killed him."

Small Badger translated. Motomo had him ask the most obvious question. "Why them follow you?"

"I don't know," Fargo admitted. "I aim to find out, though. Once I do, Motomo is welcome to them."

Motomo said something that brought a flash of anger from Small Badger.

"Him ask if I think you speak with straight tongue. I tell him you always speak with straight tongue."

That wasn't entirely true. Fargo would bend the truth when it suited him.

Throughout the afternoon he noticed Motomo giving him thoughtful looks. That evening when they made camp the aggrieved father didn't glare as he usually did.

Fargo got a good night's rest. He had the last watch. As he was putting his coffee on just before sunrise he looked to the northeast and saw a bright spot of reddish-orange miles off. It was another campfire. Since Speckled Wolf and his friends had been heading southeast, Fargo reasoned it must be someone else. Hostiles, possibly. He mentioned it to the Nez Perce when they woke up.

Small Badger wanted to go see who it was. "They near our land. Maybe they enemies."

"What if you're right?" Fargo sought to dissuade him. "Say it's a war party with twenty or thirty warriors?"

"That not be good."

"It'd be even worse if they spot us."

"We be smart and not be seen."

"It's too risky," Fargo said. "Let sleeping dogs lie."

"You think they have dogs?"

"It's another white expression," Fargo explained. "It means you should never go around asking for trouble."

"I ever say how strange whites talk?"

Fargo wasn't done arguing. "Didn't that fight with the Blackfeet teach you anything? We tangle with another war party and we could end up dead."

"How about just one go and see who they be."

"Let's not stir up a hornet's nest if we don't have to."

"Now they bugs?"

Fargo chuckled and reached for the coffeepot. He noticed that the Ovaro was staring intently into the trees with its ear pricked, and he swiveled to see why. "Damn."

Well off in the deep predawn shadows sat a rider. An Indian. The instant Fargo spotted him, he reined around and used his heels on his mount.

"Something the matter?" Small Badger asked.

"We just got stung."

12

Fargo was careful to stay well back to keep from being spotted. He never rode into the open if he could help it. For half an hour he trailed the warrior until the tracks brought him to a sawtooth ridge. He caught the scent of wood smoke. Drawing rein, he swung down, shucked the Henry, and stalked to a point that overlooked a winding valley. The warrior he had followed was almost to the bottom.

Other warriors waited for him. Fargo counted four, and was relieved. Even more so when he saw a dead buck had been slung over a horse. It was a hunting party, not a war party. Better yet, he took them to be Yakimas, allies of the Nez Perce. They posed no threat. That the warrior hadn't shown himself to Small Badger and the others was probably out of caution brought on by the presence of a white man.

Fargo mounted and headed back. He took his time. He'd told Small Badger to keep going and he would catch up. Motomo, for once, didn't object. It felt great to be shed of them. He couldn't wait to deliver the Appaloosas and get on with his life.

The Nez Perce had not gone far. On a switchback Fargo drew rein and leaned on the saddle horn and watched them. It was nice to enjoy a few more minutes alone. Out of habit he scanned the slopes across the valley, and stiffened. Three horsemen were paralleling the Nez Perce, high up near the tree line.

Fargo could guess who they were—Speckled Wolf, Rooster

and Ferret Killer. He'd figured they were long gone by now but he was wrong. When they filed in among dense firs and were out of sight, he reined down the mountain, riding hard.

Barely a quarter of a mile separated the mountain he had descended from the mountain the breeds were on. He circled around rather than expose himself, pushing the Ovaro to a gallop. He hoped the breeds were so intent on the Nez Perce that they wouldn't spot him.

Once he was in among heavy pines Fargo slowed and reined up the slope. He had a long climb ahead. He imagined that Small Badger must be wondering what was keeping him but it couldn't be helped. He needed answers and this time he was going to get them.

The tree line was so high up that when he reached it, the Nez Perce and their horses looked like ants. Fresh hoofprints showed that the breeds weren't far ahead. With wary care Fargo closed on his quarry. He avoided patches of loose rock that might clatter and give him away. And there they were.

Fargo reined into cover. When they stopped so did he. Rooster pointed at the Nez Perce and said something and Speckled Wolf nodded. The three of them then angled down the mountain.

Wondering what they were up to, Fargo followed. They were making for the Nez Perce. Or rather for the end of the valley, apparently seeking to reach it before the Nez Perce did. An ambush, Fargo figured, and rode faster.

The afternoon was waning. In another hour or so the sun would set and the Nez Perce would make camp. Fargo suspected the breeds intended to wait until then to strike.

Now and then he caught sight of Small Badger and the others. Motomo was leading Thunderhoof and the mare.

A belt of firs opened onto a steeper slope sprinkled with spruce. Fargo had lost sight of the breeds and kept rising in the stirrups to try to spot them. He rounded a blue spruce and started to rise, and swore.

Not thirty feet away stood Ferret Killer. He was off his horse, examining a front hoof.

It was hard to say which of them was more surprised. Fargo instantly drew rein but the harm had been done. Ferret Killer hollered and brought his rifle up, an older percussion model, the stock decorated with brass studs. Fargo reined behind a spruce just as the rifle boomed. Vaulting down, he peered between the branches.

He thought Ferret Killer might come after him, but no, the man was on his bay and racing to catch up to his companions.

Fargo swung onto the Ovaro and jabbed his spurs. He rounded tree after tree. He rounded yet another and a blow to the chest lifted him clear out of the saddle. He feared for a moment he had been shot but he didn't hear the crack of a rifle or pistol and then he was on his back, the breath knocked out of him, his chest a welter of pain.

Over him loomed Ferret Killer. The breed had dismounted and waited for him and swung the rifle like a club.

Ferret Killer drew his knife.

Fargo rolled as the blade flashed down. Ferret Killer stabbed at his chest but a sweep of Fargo's leg sent the half-breed tumbling. They were both on their feet in a heartbeat, Ferret Killer's knife gleaming in the sunlight. Fargo drew his Colt.

"Drop it or die."

Ferret Killer hesitated but only until he heard the click of the hammer. The knife fell to the grass and he raised his arms. "Go ahead and shoot, white-eye. I am ready to die."

"Good for you," Fargo said. "But first I want some answers. What are you and your friends up to? Why did you follow me all this way?"

"Haven't you guessed? To stop you from buying the Appaloosas."

"The same question. Why?"

"If I told you it would make no difference."

"Make more sense than that."

Ferret Killer glanced down the mountain and then stared at the Colt. "You will kill me whether I answer or not so go ahead and get it over with."

Fargo took a gamble. He lowered the hammer and twirled the Colt into his holster. "There. Now will you tell me?"

"Is this a trick?" Ferret Killer asked in some amazement.

"I want to know what the hell is going on."

"Very well. I will—"

Ferret Killer got no further. The undergrowth crackled and out of it crashed Speckled Wolf and Rooster. Both jerked rifles to their shoulders and took swift aim.

Fargo flung himself behind a spruce. Only Rooster's rifle boomed, and he missed. Quickly, Fargo snaked out his Colt. More crashing and crackling told him the breeds were fleeing. He darted out but didn't have a clear shot. The Ovaro had stopped a stone's throw away and he ran to it and vaulted into the saddle. Jabbing his boots into the stirrups, he gave chase.

Fargo was confident he could catch them. Few horses were as fast as the Ovaro; fewer still had its stamina. But the slope was so steep he couldn't ride flat out. He had to hold the pinto in for its own sake. The half-breeds were more reckless. As a result, he lost ground.

Fargo was fit to be tied. Nothing seemed to go right of late. He kept the three in sight until without warning they seemed to be swallowed by the earth. A dry wash was the reason. They had ridden down into it and raced away along the bottom. He stayed after them, the Ovaro's heavy hoofs churning clods of dirt. He went around several bends and couldn't understand why he didn't see them. Then he glanced down and wanted to howl in frustration.

There were no tracks.

Fargo reined around. He knew what he would find before he found it. They had left the gully and he had missed it. Cleverly, they had done it at a bend.

He went up and over and pursued them into dense forest. He had lost precious time and now they were farther ahead than ever.

Fargo chased them for two miles and finally had to rein in. The Ovaro was lathered with sweat and growing winded. He had been outwitted and left to eat their dust. His chance to find out the truth had slipped away.

Angry at himself, Fargo headed down the mountain. He wasn't in any hurry. As a result, the sun was almost down when he came on the Nez Perce. They had chosen a large clearing by a narrow stream for their camp. Kicking Bird was watering the horses. Small Badger was kindling the fire. Motomo had brought down a rabbit with an arrow and was butchering it. None of them noticed him until he entered the clearing.

Small Badger was delighted he had made it back safe. Fargo related what had happened and Kicking Bird asked the question, through Small Badger, that was plaguing Fargo.

"What these half-breeds want? Why they follow us?"

Fargo didn't know. Speckled Wolf and his friends weren't out to steal the Appaloosas; they were out to stop him from delivering them to Clarence Bell.

Why, was anyone's guess.

That night, as usual, they took turns keeping watch. Fargo had from about midnight to two. He sat by the fire and listened to the cacophony of bestial cries and screams and roars and came to a couple of conclusions. First, that Bell and the breeds must be enemies. Second, that the breeds weren't killers. Initially, they had tried to steal the Ovaro rather than kill him. Speckled Wolf had shot Running Elk in self-defense. Ferret Killer had tried to kill him but that was because he was after him.

Whatever their motive for wanting to stop him, Fargo had taken half the payment and promised to see the job through, and he was a man of his word.

Kicking Bird relieved him.

Fargo lay on his back, propped on his saddle, his blanket

to his chest, and tried to sleep. Once again it proved elusive. He tossed and shifted from side to side and finally succumbed.

The next day they were on the lookout for the half-breeds but saw no sign of them. The same with the day after. Fargo was sure Speckled Wolf and his friends were still out there and still shadowing them but they had learned from their mistake and were being extra vigilant not to be caught.

Fargo and the Nez Perce took turns leading Thunderhoof and the mare. He grew fond of the stallion. It was the one horse he'd come across that he admired almost as much as he did the Ovaro.

Appaloosas were a fine breed. They were noted for their calm dispositions as well as their keen intelligence. Their endurance was exceptional. Besides which, the manner in which Thunderhoof carried himself, the way he stood and moved, showed that here was no ordinary horse. Thunderhoof was notches above the common herd, an animal that any man who knew anything about horses would be proud to own.

The mare was mild and easy to handle. At night she stood by the stallion's side. During the day she meekly followed him.

Four days after Fargo's clash with the breeds, the Nez Perce climbed a series of benches toward a pass. Fargo was leading the Appaloosas. When he glimpsed movement higher up he thought it must be Speckled Wolf and his friends. All he saw was a shadowy bulk that he mistook for a horse. Then a shaft of sunlight splashed brown fur and he knew it for what it was, and he called out a warning.

The Nez Perce stopped and looked back at him and Fargo raised his arm and pointed.

A grizzly had lumbered out of the firs. As big as buffalo, with pronounced humps and massive heads, grizzlies were the lords of the Rockies. Vicious claws and razor teeth rendered them supreme shredding machines. Normally grizzlies shied from humans but this one was curious. It stared and raised its nose to the wind and sniffed.

Fargo swore. It could be the grizzly was hungry and was

trying to figure out if they were something it would like to eat.

Small Badger was notching an arrow to his bowstring.

"Don't even think it," Fargo warned.

"Eh?"

"You'll only make him mad."

Grizzlies were enormously difficult to kill. Their thick bones, their heavy layers of muscle and fat, were virtually bullet- and arrow-proof.

"But what if him attack?"

"Let's hope to hell he doesn't." Fargo started to reach for the Henry but thought better of it. He must hold on to the lead rope and be ready to get out of there.

The grizzly did more sniffing.

"Sometimes bears run when people yell," Small Badger mentioned. "You want I yell?"

"Give it a try," Fargo said. He had used the same trick himself. Black bears nearly always turned tail. Grizzlies were more unpredictable.

Cupping a hand to his mouth, Small Badger let out with a war whoop that rolled down off the mountain.

The bear rumbled deep in its chest.

"Don't do that again," Fargo cautioned.

Kicking Bird said something to Small Badger and slapped his legs against his mount and moved toward the patriarch of the wilds.

"What the hell is he doing?"

"Him say he lead bear off."

"Stop him."

"Do not worry, Iron Will. He very good rider and have quick horse. He know what to do."

"He'll provoke it," Fargo said.

Suddenly the grizzly reared onto its hind legs. Its maw parted and it let out with a roar.

Kicking Bird kept on going.

"Call him back," Fargo urged Small Badger.

"It do no good. Him can do what he want."

Fargo's gut churned. Every instinct he had told him this was a mistake and his instincts were seldom wrong. "Do it for me. Tell him to stop and let the bear wander off on its own."

Small Badger called up to the other warrior. Kicking Bird glanced down at them and kept on climbing.

"Damn it."

The bear dropped onto all fours and charged.

13

Small Badger was right. Kicking Bird *was* a good rider and his horse *was* quick. He reined around and used his heels and his mount exploded into motion.

So did the grizzly. And grizzlies, for all their immense size and huge bulk, were incredibly swift. Over short distances they were as fast as a horse, or faster. This grizzly, although enormous, had the speed of a cougar. It was on Kicking Bird so swiftly the warrior had no time to react.

A giant paw slashed. Red streamers spewed and a squeal of agony was torn from the horse. Down it crashed. Just in time, Kicking Bird threw himself clear.

The grizzly could easily have finished both off but instead it ran past them and locked its eyes on the first thing it saw.

"Oh hell." Fargo wheeled the Ovaro, hauled on the lead rope, and fled down the mountain. Thunderhoof and the mare pounded after him.

So did the bear. A mighty roar and a burst of muscle and it was almost on top of the mare.

Fargo threw caution aside. To save the Appaloosas he must ride like a madman. He glanced back and saw the grizzly gnash at the mare's tail. Its teeth missed by inches.

Small Badger was shouting but Fargo couldn't hear him over the din of pounding hooves. A Douglas fir reared and he swept around it, clipping a branch. Thunderhoof and the mare were right on the Ovaro's flanks. Fargo realized that should he suddenly stop they would plow into him and all three animals would go down with the bear there to rip and rend.

Small Badger and Motomo were galloping after them but there was nothing the two Nez Perce could do. Their arrows would only enrage the bear more.

Fargo knuckled down for the ride of his life. He reined right, he reined left, avoiding obstacle after obstacle Thunderhoof and the mare matched the Ovaro's every move, their manes flying.

The grizzly didn't relent. It pressed after them, snapping and growling, a living behemoth of destruction, an embodiment of all that was savage and primal in the wild.

A boulder the size of a covered wagon hove out of the earth. Fargo swept around it and had to jerk on the reins to avoid another, smaller boulder directly in his path. Thunderhoof vaulted over it. The mare, pulled off-balance by the rope, narrowly missed breaking her legs.

The bear raked a paw and the mare squealed.

Fargo spied a thicket of brambles. Blackberries, so delicious to eat, the plants lined with sharp thorns that tore at any man or beast that ate them. He rode straight for it. At the last possible split second he reined to the right and once again Thunderhoof and the mare imitated the Ovaro as if they were living shadows.

The grizzly snapped at the mare as she turned, and missed. Unable to stop, it hurtled into the briars. Its fur and thick hide protected it from the worst of the thorns but not all of them, and in a frenzy of rage it tore at the source of its hurt.

Fargo was able to increase his lead but not by much. The bear was after them within moments, its fury lending it added speed.

The slope grew steeper but Fargo couldn't slow, couldn't stop. Leaning back, he thrust his boots against the stirrups. The rope grew slack. Thunderhoof was almost next to the Ovaro, the mare only a little behind.

Fargo risked another glance. The grizzly was almost on

top of them. He faced front just in time to see a log. As thick around as his hips, one end lay on top of a boulder a good three feet off the ground. It gave him an idea. He used the same trick he had with the brambles. He waited until the last possible instant and hauled on the reins. The Ovaro and the Appaloosas veered aside barely in time.

The grizzly was a shade slow in perceiving its peril. It slammed into the log with the impact of a runaway wagon, a thousand pounds of sinew and bone and fat moving at thirty miles an hour. Its momentum catapulted it into a tumbling roll that carried it dozens of yards down the slope. In a cloud of dust and bits of debris, the giant bear slid to a stop and rose groggily to its four paws.

Fargo saw it all. He quickly reined back up the mountain, seeking to put as much distance behind him as he could in case the bear came after them.

The grizzly stood looking around as if in confusion. It gazed up at Fargo and the fleeing horses, uttered another roar, and went off down the mountain, presumably to find easier prey.

Fargo didn't stop until he met the Nez Perce coming down.

"You all right!" Small Badger exclaimed in relief. "I much worried bear kill you."

"You weren't the only one." Fargo patted the Ovaro and climbed down to examine Thunderhoof and the mare. Neither, amazingly, were any the worse for their hairsbreadth escape.

Kicking Bird was back on his horse. Other than deep furrows in its flank, the animal was unscathed.

Motomo addressed Small Badger, who translated.

"Him say what you do very brave. Him say only man who cares for horses try so hard to save them."

"He keeps giving me compliments, I'm liable to blush."

Small Badger blinked, and then laughed. He translated, and for the first time since they met, Fargo made Motomo smile.

The grizzly was almost out of sight. Small Badger stared after it and summed up their encounter with, "We lucky, yes?"

"Lucky as hell," Fargo said.

They rested and pushed on. Toward sunset they stopped high on a broad shelf with a spectacular vista of the country ahead. Supper consisted of coffee and dried rabbit meat left over from the night before.

Motomo had been quiet all afternoon. Now he turned to Small Badger and went on for a good long spell.

"He want me tell you maybe him make mistake. Maybe you not have bad heart like he think you do."

Fargo bit into a chunk of rabbit and chewed. "He doesn't want me dead anymore?"

"He good father, Iron Will. He love son very much. When Running Elk killed, it wound him here." Small Badger touched a hand to his chest over his heart. "It like part of him ripped out. You understand what he mean?"

"I savvy," Fargo acknowledged. He'd never had a kid of his own but he'd heard folks say that losing one was a torment like no other.

"He think only that you to blame. He think only son must be avenged. Is that right word? Avenged?"

"It will do until a better word comes along."

"What? Oh. That joke, yes?"

"Tell Motomo I'm grateful," Fargo directed. Not having to worry about getting a knife in the back might help him sleep better.

Small Badger was gnawing on his lower lip. "Iron Will, it all right I ask you something?"

"We're pards, aren't we?"

"Were you afraid when bear was after you?"

"Scared as hell," Fargo admitted.

"But you not show it."

"I was too busy trying to stay alive. A month from now I'll probably break down with the shakes."

"I hope I brave like you if bear ever come after me," Small Badger said sincerely.

Fargo told himself he should be used to it. Life in the wild was fraught with dangers, each a reminder that no one ever knew which day would be their last.

He'd learned not to dwell on the close shaves. A man could lose his nerve that way.

No, the smart thing to do was shut them from the mind.

Over the next hour the Nez Perce made small talk. Fargo listened with half an ear, his interest perking when Motomo suggested that one of them should look around for sign of enemies.

"Two should go," Fargo amended. "Each can watch the other's back."

Small Badger stood. "I do it. Who want come with me?"

Fargo would as soon stay and drink coffee but the young warrior was his friend. "Count me in."

Around them the twilight darkened. Soon night would fall.

Fargo made for the shelf rim thirty feet away, Small Badger trying to match his long strides.

"All right I ask you another question?"

"So long as it's not personal."

"What that be?"

"Things like how many women I've bedded or how many men I've had to buck out in gore."

"Oh. I not ask that," Small Badger assured him. "I want know why you make my cousin so sad."

"Your cousin?"

"Many Clouds."

Fargo stopped in his tracks. "Hell in a basket. Why didn't either of you tell me? She never once mentioned she was related."

"Maybe she think not important," Small Badger said. "Her father my father's brother."

"That makes her kin to the chief. I'd say that's important enough to let a man know."

"My father not mind. Him say she be grown woman and you be grown man."

"A wise gent, your pa."

"I hope him do right to sell m'a min to rancher. Some Nimipuu not like it. They want only Nimipuu breed m'a min."

"It should work out all right," Fargo hedged. He wasn't the one to judge, especially as he had a stake in getting the Appaloosas there. He came to the edge and peered down. Below, the forest canopy stretched for as far as the eye could see.

"I like to be bird," Small Badger said.

"How's that again?"

The young warrior flapped his arms. "So I fly over trees and over mountains and see all there is to see."

"That's some imagination you have."

"Imagi-what?"

"It means you're good at coming up with notions in that noggin of yours," Fargo explained.

"Notions. Noggin," Small Badger repeated, and grinned. "White men tongue strange as white people."

"Most whites would say the same about you and yours." It had been Fargo's experience that few bothered to learn Indian languages because they wanted nothing to do with Indians.

Fargo scoured the dark expanse for the telltale glimmer of a campfire. He wondered if maybe the breeds had given up. Whatever they were up to, maybe they had decided it wasn't worth it.

"No fire," Small Badger confirmed.

Fargo turned to go back. Out of the corner of his eye he registered movement—someone rising up out of the tall grass—and he spun.

Speckled Wolf had the muzzle of his Sharps pressed to Small Badger's temple. "Twitch a muscle and he dies."

Fargo turned to stone.

"Smart man," Speckled Wolf mocked him. "Now I want you to listen, and listen good. My friends have rifles trained on the other two at the fire. A yell from me and both are dead."

"Why you do this?" Small Badger asked.

"Did I say you could talk, boy?" Speckled Wolf jabbed

him with the barrel. "I don't want to hear a peep out of you. This is between me and your friend, here. He's the one Bell is paying. He's the one who doesn't give a damn about your tribe or your horses."

"He be our friend," Small Badger proudly declared.

"There you go again. Another word, and so help me I'll split your damn skull."

Fargo willed himself to stay calm. If the breed wanted them dead, he'd have shot them already. "What *do* you want?"

"The Appaloosas. Throw a rope over them and bring them here and put the rope in my hands and this boy and the other two live out the night. Try anything, anything at all, and I swear we'll blow their brains out."

"So you're nothing but horse thieves," Fargo stalled.

"Call it what you want but Bell isn't getting his hands on that stallion and mare. I don't have a lick of Nez Perce blood in me but I'll be damned if I'll let that happen."

"It would help if you would explain what this is all about."

"You're wasting time," Speckled Wolf said. "Get the damn horses. If those other two want to know what you're doing, make up some excuse." He nodded at Small Badger. "Remember. One squeeze and the boy won't have much left from the neck up."

"I not boy," Small Badger said.

"Hush, you dimwit." Speckled Wolf gestured toward the campfire.

"Better hurry. This boy might try something stupid and I'll have to kill him anyway."

The same thought had occurred to Fargo. Holding his hands where Speckled Wolf could see them, he backed away. "I'm going. Give me five minutes."

"You have two."

Motomo and Kicking Bird were by the fire, talking. Fargo walked past them and over to the Appaloosas. He pulled out the picket pins and got the lead rope and looped it over Thunderhoof and then over the mare. As he was about to walk off,

Motomo and Kicking Bird rose and came over. Motomo gestured at the Appaloosas and then at Fargo as if to ask, "What are you doing?"

Fargo had no time to explain. He went to go around.

That was when Kicking Bird stepped in front of him and put his hand on the hilt of his knife.

14

Fargo resorted to sign language. He signed simply, "Move."

Kicking Bird took his hand off his knife to sign back, "Question. Where you go?"

Fargo signed, "Must hurry," and again went to go around. Once more Kicking Bird moved in front of him.

Motomo appeared confused. "Question. Why you take horses?"

Fargo was wasting precious seconds. Speckled Wolf had only given him two minutes. He tried a different tack. He signed, "I speak future time." There was no sign for "later" in the way the term was used by whites. He started to lead the horses off.

Kicking Bird and Motomo exchanged looks and Kicking Bird did as he had done before.

His fingers flying, Fargo signed, "Half-breed have Small Badger. Kill quick I no go."

The two Nez Perce showed their shock. Fargo gripped the lead rope and took a step and Kicking Bird moved to block him but Motomo gripped Kicking Bird's arm and pulled him back. Kicking Bird resisted but only for a moment. He stopped and motioned for Fargo to keep going.

Fargo thought it prudent to sign, "Stay here. Half-breed shoot Small Badger you go." Thankfully, the two warriors had the presence of mind to listen. But Kicking Bird fingered his knife hilt.

It had taken more than two minutes but no shots rang out.

Fargo found Speckled Wolf and Small Badger where he had left them and held out the lead rope.

"Glad you didn't shoot him."

Speckled Wolf motioned toward the campfire. "I saw them try to stop you. And I don't want this boy dead. I want the Appaloosas."

"I'd like to know what this is all about."

"You are not to blame for any of it," Speckled Wolf told him. Taking the rope, he backed away, his Sharps trained on Small Badger. "Don't follow us. If you do you or us will die."

"You can't expect to get away with this," Fargo said.

"We do what we have to. You would understand if you had been born like me, half and half. It is the red half of me doing this. The white half would just let him do it."

"Let who do what? I don't savvy."

"I don't have time to explain." Speckled Wolf was a silhouette in the gathering darkness. "Heed me, scout. Don't come after us. It is best for you and it is best for us and most of all it's best for these two horses. I would shoot them rather than let you take them to Clarence Bell."

"Do you know him?"

"Better than you do."

On that puzzling note, the breed melted into the night, taking Thunderhoof and the mare.

Small Badger reached for an arrow in his quiver and took a step. "Come. We catch before he go far."

Fargo grabbed his wrist. "You heard him. They'll kill the horses. Is that what you want?"

"We not let him take them," Small Badger insisted. "Must stop any way we can."

"We have to do it smart. We can't go rushing off." Fargo gazed into the dark. "We'll wait until morning. The tracks will be fresh. They can't possibly lose us."

Small Badger was trying to tug free but stopped. "All right. I not like but we do as you want." He paused. "Why you think they take m'a min? What this all mean?"

"I wish to hell I knew."

Motomo and Kicking Bird listened to Small Badger's account in growing anger. A heated dispute took place. Kicking Bird was mad that they hadn't tried to stop the horse thieves and wanted to go after them right that instant. It took some persuading to calm him enough for him to see reason.

Fargo hunkered by the fire and sipped coffee. There was nothing he could do until daylight. He went over everything Speckled Wolf had said and could come to no conclusions other than he was more certain than ever the half-breeds weren't killers. They weren't renegades. They weren't *bad* men. Which made what they were doing all the more mystifying.

Small Badger squatted across from him. "They say they do as you want but Kicking Bird not happy. Him think we do wrong letting them have horses."

"He'd rather you were shot?"

"No. But my father tell him to keep m'a min safe. He feel . . . responsible. That is good word, yes?"

"I don't aim to let them get away with it," Fargo enlightened him. "We'll catch them. But when we do, I don't want them killed."

"They steal Appaloosas, they die."

"Don't you want to know why? I sure do. They didn't take the Appaloosas for themselves or to sell for money. There's something else going on here."

"They are breeds. They not think like we do."

Long ago Fargo had learned that whites weren't the only ones who looked down their noses at those with mixed blood. A lot of Indians did the same. "They're men like you and me."

Small Badger swapped words with the other two, and then said, "All right. We be patient. We let you find out why they take m'a min. Then we kill them."

Fargo slept surprisingly soundly. He was up well before sunrise and had the Ovaro saddled and ready.

The three Nez Perce were glum. Kicking Bird, in particular, was in a foul temper and anxious to be off.

The trail was plain as a trail could be. Fargo started at the rim and read the sign as he went.

Speckled Wolf had led Thunderhoof and the mare into the trees. There he had been joined by Rooster and Ferret Killer. All three climbed on their mounts and headed to the southeast, the last rider leading the Appaloosas.

Fargo hoped he would come on where the breeds had camped for the night but they had pushed on through. Speckled Wolf knew the Nez Perce would be after them and was trying to get as far ahead as possible. Not that it would do him any good. Unless there was another storm, the breeds were as good as caught. Fargo reckoned on overtaking them by the middle of the afternoon, if not sooner.

Small Badger, for once, had little to say until Fargo stopped about midday to rest their animals. Pacing back and forth, he complained, "Father be mad at me if we lose Thunderhoof and mare. I not be good son in his eyes."

"We'll get them back," Fargo vowed.

"That not all we do. Breeds must die."

"You're getting awful bloodthirsty in your young age."

Small Badger stopped pacing. "It more than that. My people have many enemies. Enemies who want take our land if they think we not protect what is ours."

"No one will ever know but us," Fargo said, but his young friend wasn't listening.

"Nimipuu must be strong. When enemies come our country, we drive off. When enemies raid our villages, we raid them. When enemies kill Nimipuu, Nimipuu kill enemies."

Fargo didn't press the point. Arguing would be useless. No tribe would let their horses be stolen or one of their own be killed and not seek vengeance.

Climbing back on the Ovaro, he took up the hunt.

The sun crawled high on its westward arc. Around them the woodland abounded with game. Deer bolted with tails erect. Chipmunks chattered from rocky nooks. A startled grouse took wing, the beat of its wing loud in the thin mountain air.

It was past two when Fargo drew rein on the rim of a tableland. A mile below were three riders. The first man led two horses with familiar markings.

"It them!" Small Badger cried, and raised his reins to give pursuit.

Fargo wheeled the Ovaro in front of his mount. "Not so fast. I want your word first."

"My word?" Small Badger repeated in puzzlement.

"Yours and theirs," Fargo said with a nod at Motomo and Kicking Bird.

"I want your promise you won't kill them unless it can't be helped."

"We already agree not to kill them until you find out what you want to know."

"Remind them."

Motomo asked something and Small Badger replied. Both Motomo and Kicking Bird looked angrily at Fargo and Motomo said something else.

"He say he do as you want but he not happy."

"What about Kicking Bird?" Fargo didn't like how Kicking Bird was fingering the hilt of his knife.

Before Small Badger could translate, Kicking Bird reined sharply away and galloped after the distant figures. Small Badger called to him but Kicking Bird didn't stop.

"Hell." Fargo resorted to his spurs. He had been afraid it would come to this. Unless he could catch Kicking Bird, blood would flow.

After him pounded Small Badger and Motomo.

Fargo had been doing a lot of hard riding of late but the Ovaro held up well. The stallion always did have more stamina than most. It proved it yet again by flying as if its hooves were endowed with wings. The terrain, though, was thick with trees and dotted with boulders and logs and tangles. Overtaking Kicking Bird would take hard riding.

Fargo tried his best. He called on all his experience and skill but he was still well behind Kicking Bird when Kicking

Bird broke into the open, uttered a war yell, and strung an arrow to his bowstring.

Up ahead, Speckled Wolf and his friends were in full flight. They had heard the thunder of approaching hooves and spotted the Nez Perce.

A rifle cracked. Ferret Killer had fired at Kicking Bird but missed.

Kicking Bird raised his bow.

"No!" Fargo shouted.

The shaft flashed into the vault of blue. It was an incredible shot. Rooster looked back just as the arrow caught him in the forehead. The barbed tip penetrated clean through his head and burst out the rear of his cranium. Limbs pinwheeling, he struck the ground.

Kicking Bird notched another arrow. He was guiding his mount with his legs to free his hands.

Speckled Wolf looked back. He had the lead rope and was bent low over his horse.

Fargo was in a quandary. He didn't want the breeds dead but he couldn't shoot Kicking Bird for doing what any warrior in Kicking Bird's place would do. Swearing a blue streak, he lashed the Ovaro.

Kicking Bird was gaining. He raised his bow and drew the string to his cheek.

Unexpectedly, Ferret Killer hauled on his reins and brought his sorrel to a sliding stop. In a whirl of dust he reined broadside. His hand rose from his waist holding a revolver. He aimed carefully, one eye shut, and the weapon belched smoke and lead.

Kicking Bird's head snapped back as if he had been punched. He twisted at the hips and his arm drooped and the bow fell to the grass.

Fargo flew past him and saw that a slug had caught him in the left eye; there was a hole where the eyeball should be. The body began to slide off, Kicking Bird's head flopping back and forth.

Ferret Killer had wheeled and was again seeking to escape. He reloaded as he rode, which took considerable practice.

Fargo heard a howl of fury behind him. Motomo and Small Badger had reached Kicking Bird and Motomo was shaking his lance in rage. Fargo focused on Ferret Killer, who kept glancing back.

"I'm not your enemy! I only want the Appaloosas!"

"Like hell!" Ferret Killer yelled, and pointed the revolver.

In a twinkling Fargo had swung onto the side of the Ovaro and was hanging Comanche-fashion. When no shot sounded he pulled himself high enough to see Ferret Killer riding faster than ever. It had been a trick to slow him.

Fargo swung back up. As he did a horse pounded past, the warrior on it oblivious to everything save his quarry. "Motomo!" Fargo shouted. He might as well have saved his breath.

Like an avenging swarthy angel, Motomo bore down on Ferret Killer. He would soon be in casting range. Ferret Killer must have realized as much because he suddenly brought his mount to a stop, reined around, and extended his six-shooter.

Motomo ignored the threat and raised his lance, every sinew tensed for the throw.

Ferret Killer fired. The slug cored Motomo's left shoulder and nearly unhorsed him but he clung on. His right arm blurred up and out.

Fargo saw it all as if in slow motion.

The lance cleaved the air, the tip glittering bright in the sunlight.

Shock registered on Ferret Killer as he sought to rein around and get out of there.

But he hadn't quite turned when the lance cleaved his side from left to right and ruptured out of him below his ribs. The force had driven it all the way through his body.

Motomo whooped in triumph.

Ferret Killer reeled and clutched at the lance, scarlet flecking his lips.

His body sagged and his head drooped. He stopped moving but didn't fall. There he sat, dead in the saddle.

Fargo figured that Motomo would stop.

Not so.

Motomo whipped his knife from his sheath, jabbed his heels, and flew after Speckled Wolf.

Cursing, Fargo pressed after them.

15

Fargo intended to stop Motomo if he could. Speckled Wolf was the only one left who could tell him why the breeds had taken the Appaloosas. He began to gain but Motomo was also gaining.

Speckled Wolf kept looking back. He was tugging on the lead rope and riding as fast as his horse could gallop but it was plain he couldn't hope to get away. Perhaps that was why he suddenly hauled on his reins. Twisting in the saddle, he jammed his Sharps to his shoulder.

"Motomo!" Fargo shouted, hoping against hope the warrior would stop. He didn't want him slain, either.

But Motomo had lost his son and he was almost upon the man responsible.

Instead of stopping he raised his knife and gave voice to a war whoop.

The Sharps boomed.

Motomo was smashed back but somehow stayed on. Grabbing his mount's mane, he straightened. He swept past the mare and past Thunderhoof and was next to Speckled Wolf. The knife flashed. Then Motomo was past and pitching from his horse.

By the time Fargo got there Speckled Wolf was on the ground, too, doubled over. Fargo vaulted from the saddle. One glance at Motomo was enough; the slug had ripped through his sternum and exploded out of his body between his shoulder blades. His eyes were wide and empty. That he had lived

111

long enough to stab Speckled Wolf was a testament to the power of human hate.

Speckled Wolf had dropped the Sharps but still had a revolver and was trying to draw it.

Covering him with the Colt, Fargo warned, "I don't want to kill you if I don't have to."

Speckled Wolf's teeth were clenched. His other hand was on the hilt of the knife jutting from his body. Wisely, he hadn't tried to pull it out. If he did, he might die within moments from blood loss. "I am already dead."

Fargo sank to one knee and relieved him of the revolver. He could tell by the angle the knife had penetrated that the wound was mortal. "He was the father of the boy you killed."

"I know," Speckled Wolf said, his lips flecked with red drops. "A good man. I do not blame him."

"You're the strangest horse thief I ever met."

The pain made Speckled Wolf groan. "There is something I must tell you . . ." he started to say.

The hammering of hooves heralded Small Badger arrival. He leaped from his horse and raised his bow.

Fargo shifted between them. "No."

"He must die!"

"Look at him," Fargo said. "He's already dead."

"He shoot Motomo!"

"Look at him, damn it."

Small Badger did, his arms slowly lowering. "Why you do this? After all him do?"

"I need answers." Fargo turned to Speckled Wolf. "What is it you were about to say?"

Speckled Wolf didn't answer.

"Why did you take the Appaloosas?" Fargo put a hand on his shoulder. "What were you up to?"

Speckled Wolf's head drooped. His body went limp and his hands slid to the ground and he exhaled a last long breath and was gone.

"Hell in a basket," Fargo said.

"He be dead?" Small Badger came closer. "Good. He deserve to die. He kill two Nimipuu."

Fargo sighed in frustration. Now he would never know what brought all this on. He stood and went to Thunderhoof and the mare and examined them. Neither was the worse for the chase.

"We bury my friends," Small Badger said sadly.

"We'll plant all of them."

They were the rest of the day at it. To dig, they used broken limbs and their hands. Fargo wanted to pile rocks on top to discourage scavengers but there weren't many to be had.

Small Badger hardly said a word. Not until Fargo had a fire going and was putting coffee on and the sun was half gone.

"I sorry I so mad."

"Can't blame you," Fargo said.

Small Badger stared at the mounds of earth. "They die so quick. It over before I can think."

"That's how it usually is." Fargo had taken part in more violent deaths than he cared to remember.

"Now we take Thunderhoof and mare to rancher?"

"That was the plan. We'll hand them over and you'll get the rest of the money you're due and I'll get the rest of mine and then it's on to Denver for me. I aim to stay drunk for a month."

"You like whiskey a lot, yes?"

"It helps a man forget."

"Forget what?"

Fargo nodded at the graves.

"Oh."

Fargo opened his saddlebags and took out his bundle of pemmican. He offered a piece to Small Badger but the young warrior motioned that he wasn't hungry. Fargo chewed without tasting it.

"You ever wonder when maybe you die?"

Fargo shrugged. "Why worry about it? A man never knows when his time will come. When it happens, it happens, and there isn't a damn thing you can do about it."

"It not right," Small Badger said. "We born. We live. We die. Why life that way?"

"How would I know? I'm just passing through." Fargo gazed out over the mountains. "I remember the time I came across a wagon in the middle of nowhere. I wasn't much older than you. The man had been butchered and scalped. The woman had been raped and gutted. They'd had a baby. Not more than five or six months old, I'd reckon. I found it by the wagon. Someone had dashed its brains out against the wheel."

"Death ugly," Small Badger said.

"That was the day I decided this world makes no kind of sense. The day I made up my mind to live as I damn well please and the rest of the world be hanged. I don't bother anyone and I require that they don't bother me. That's all I know worth knowing."

"There be many whites like you?"

"Some. Most are content to go from their ma's womb to the grave doing what they're told to do and thinking what they're told to think. That's the sense they make of life."

"You never talk like this before."

"Hell," Fargo said. "A man can think himself in circles if he's not careful." He chuckled. "Give me a friendly filly and a bottle of coffin varnish and a card game, and that's as good as life gets."

Around them the shadows darkened and the sky went from gray to black. Howls broke the stillness. A roar filled the night. Somewhere an animal shrieked a death cry.

Fargo turned in early. The stirring of the birds at the crack of dawn brought him out of his blankets and they were soon under way.

The next several days passed without incident. On the fourth afternoon Small Badger brought down a doe with his bow and they ate until they were gorged.

Leaning back, Small Badger patted his stomach. "My belly so big I could have baby."

Fargo laughed.

Small Badger related how his father taught him to ride and shoot and how he once shot another boy in the foot by accident. "Arrow nick him so he all right. But other Nimipuu begin call me Shoots In Foot."

"You're lucky the name didn't stick," Fargo joked. His grin faded when the Ovaro and the Appaloosas raised their heads and Thunderhoof nickered.

"They smell or hear something," Small Badger stated the obvious.

Fargo grabbed the Henry and stood. They were in a clearing in a vast forest. Anything, or anyone, could be out there. He took a few steps and a tingle ran down his spine.

A pair of eyes, glowing with fire shine, was fixed on them with fierce intensity. Their size and their shape identified the creature as surely as if it were broad daylight.

"Mountain lion," Fargo warned.

Small Badger jumped up and strung an arrow. "I see it."

"Stand still. Maybe it will let us be."

Drawn by the scent of blood, the big cat was interested in the dead deer.

Fargo could have shot it but cougars rarely attacked people and he never killed an animal unless he had cause. He wasn't one of those who went around shooting things for the hell of it.

The eyes blinked and the cat stepped into the circle of firelight, its tawny body slunk low to the ground, its long tail twitching.

"Iron Will?"

"No."

The mountain lion glanced at each of them and then at the doe. They had cut off a haunch and the rest was intact. It took another couple of steps.

"Now I can?"

115

"Hush, damn it."

The cat growled and curled its thin lips, baring razor fangs.

"Please, Iron Will."

Fargo fired. He shot into the ground in front of the cougar and a geyser of dirt spattered its paws and face. Instantly, the big cat whirled and bounded off, moving so swiftly it was a tawny blur. "Happy now?"

Small Badger slowly lowered his bow. "Why you not just kill it?"

"I've already ate and I don't have any use for its hide." Fargo worked the Henry, feeding a new cartridge into the chamber.

"What if it be grizzly?"

"I'd run like hell."

Fargo spent the next hour cutting the rest of the meat into strips and setting them to dry over a frame he rigged from tree limbs. The rest of the remains he buried to discourage meat-eaters like the cougar.

Tranquil days ensued. Long hours of riding followed by tranquil nights of rest.

Fargo was in no particular hurry. It made no sense to ride the horses into the ground. They would get there when they got here.

Gradually Small Badger's mood lightened. By the eighth morning after their clash with the breeds he was his old self. "When I little I like see shapes in clouds. One time cloud like beaver. Another time cloud like fish." He pointed at one high in the vault of blue. "See that one? What it look like to you?"

"A cloud."

"No. What else?"

"A chipmunk."

Small Badger's face furrowed. "I think it look like turtle. See shell? And head and feet?"

"You're the chipmunk," Fargo said. "You chatter a man's ears off."

Small Badger grinned. "My father say I born talking."

"I believe it."

Fargo looked back at Thunderhoof and the mare, and sobered. On a ridge to the south riders had appeared. "Quick," he said, pointing. "Into the trees."

He gave the lead rope a sharp pull.

Oaks closed about them. Fargo peered up through the canopy, Nine warriors, all told, heading west. They were too far off to tell if they wore war paint.

"You think they see us?"

"Doesn't look like it."

"More Blackfeet maybe?"

"More likely Shoshones. Or maybe Crows." Both were friendly but Fargo knew of a few instances where the Crows had helped themselves to horses belonging to white men so he stayed put.

That night Fargo lay on his back, pondering. It would take them a few days yet to reach the Sweetwater River country but he couldn't help thinking that the dangerous part of their trek was behind them. The rest should be a cinch.

The Sweetwater River got its start just over the Divide not far from South Pass. It flowed generally east-northeast along a series of high hills and then cut to the southeast between the Granite Mountains and the Green Mountains and on into prime cattle-raising land.

Fargo figured that was where he would find the Circle B. They were barely half a mile past the mountains when he spotted a small herd of cows and two punchers who promptly galloped toward them. He drew rein and waited.

The cowboys had their hands on their revolvers. They came to a stop and a slab of brawn with stubble and a scar looked them up and down. "What do we have here?"

"Would this be the Circle B?" Fargo asked.

"Who wants to know?"

"Our boss don't take kindly to strangers," said the other man.

Fargo reminded himself that they were only doing their job. "My name is Fargo. Clarence Bell hired me to bring these Appaloosas." He waved his hand toward Thunderhoof and the mare. "I have come a long way and I am tired. Which way to the ranch house?"

"He might have hired you to bring those horses, mister," the first puncher said, "but he sure as hell didn't hire you to bring an Injun." He put his hand on his revolver. "And if he did that's just too bad."

16

Fargo's own hand was on his hip. He saw the cowboy start to draw and palmed his Colt. In the bat of an eye it was out and cocked. At the *click* the cowboy imitated stone.

The other puncher whistled softly. "God Almighty. Did you see that, Hank? I didn't even see his hand move."

Hank was staring at the Colt like a man about to climb a gallows. His throat bobbed and he said, "Hold on there, mister. I wouldn't really have shot the redskin."

"Take your hand off your pistol, you peckerwood," Fargo snapped.

Hank obeyed, raising his arms out from his sides. "Buck me out in gore and you'll have every hand on the Circle B after you."

"How would they know I did it?"

The other puncher straightened. "Why, I'd tell them."

"You take a lot for granted," Fargo said.

The cowboy blanched. "This is between Hank and you, friend. I'm just sitting here."

"The two of you are taking us to the ranch house," Fargo commanded. "Ride side by side and keep your hands away from your hardware and you might live to get there."

"We can't leave these cows. Mr. Bell would have our heads."

"What's your handle?"

"Amos. Amos Barnes."

"The cows will be fine unless there's a blizzard and we don't usually have blizzards in the summer."

"You're a hard one, mister," Amos said.

"You don't know the half of it." Fargo was stating fact, not bragging. He motioned. "Lead the way."

"I won't forget this," Hank said.

"Shut the hell up," Amos growled at him. "If you hadn't been so damn eager we wouldn't be in this pickle."

"How far is the ranch house?" Fargo asked.

"Four hours, more or less."

"If we run into any of your friends along the way, you're to smile and wave so they think everything is fine."

The two cowboys did as they were told. Twice they passed small herds and other punchers but no one challenged them.

Fargo was mildly surprised he didn't see more cows. A ranch the size of the Circle B could graze thousands but the most he saw was about five hundred.

He idly wondered if Bell had driven a lot off to sell but didn't bother to ask the two punchers. He didn't care. All he wanted was to deliver Thunderhoof and the mare, collect his money, and be on his way.

Small Badger was unusually quiet. So much so that after a couple of hours Fargo turned to him and asked, "Cat got your tongue?"

The young warrior looked anxiously around. "Cat? Where? What kind is it?"

"That's another white expression. It means you're being awful quiet."

"Oh." Small Badger's face clouded. "I not like it here, Iron Will. This place bad medicine."

"Amos is an Indian hater. A lot of whites are like him. Don't make more of it than there is."

"This place bad medicine," Small Badger insisted.

Fargo didn't press the point. He felt a bit uneasy, himself. He blamed their reception.

Another surprise awaited him when they reached the ranch proper. The house wasn't as big as he had imagined it would be. The stable and the bunkhouse weren't painted and there was no blacksmith shop and only a few outbuildings. All in all, as ranches went it was middling.

Hank and Amos rode to the front porch and drew rein. Hardly had they stopped than the front door opened and out clomped a big man in a flannel shirt and chaps, his thumbs hooked in his belt. He looked at them and said, "You boys are off the range when you're not supposed to be."

Hank jerked a thumb at Fargo. "Blame him, Griff. He made us come."

"That's right," Amos confirmed. "He was fixing to blow out our wicks if we didn't."

Fargo remembered Jim Stoddard saying that the ranch foreman was a man named Griff Jackson. A tough hombre, Stoddard had claimed.

That tough hombre now turned toward him. "That true, mister?"

"I told them I was working for your boss and Hank, here, went for his six-shooter," Fargo elaborated. "Since I didn't figure I could trust them not to shoot me in the back, I brought them along."

"He tried to draw on you?" Griff Jackson's features hardened and he lowered his big hand to his side so that it covered a Smith and Wesson in his holster. "You were told, Hank. The boss let all of you know he was expecting this hombre."

"He has an Injun with him!" Hank bleated. "What else was I to do?"

Jackson's jaw muscles twitched. "We'll talk this out later. For now go to the bunkhouse and stay there." Both cowboys went to rein around. "Not you, Amos. I want you to go remind the rest of the boys about our guests and tell them to be damn sure not to act up or they'll answer to me."

"Yes, sir."

"Then you're to head back out on the range and watch those cattle like you're supposed to be doing. We lost a single head, it's coming out of your hide. You got me?"

"Loud and clear."

Fargo was struck by their fear; they were scared to death of this Griff Jackson. "We've come a long way," he broke in. "Is your boss to home? I'd like to get this over with."

The foreman nodded. "I'll fetch him. Climb down and stretch your legs. I won't be a minute." He clomped inside.

Fargo stayed in the saddle. "This won't take long," he assured Small Badger, who sat his horse as if he were sitting on glass. "Relax. You just heard. That puncher acted on his own."

"Maybe this be mistake."

"I never took you for a worrywart."

"Look at them," Small Badger said, and nodded.

Fargo shifted. He hadn't paid much attention to the hands. About half a dozen had been going about their daily duties. Every last one had stopped and was staring. Or, rather, *glaring*. They were looking at Small Badger as if they wanted to do as Hank had done. Before he had time to think about why, the front door opened again.

"Mr. Fargo! You made it!" Clarence Bell smiled and came off the porch and over to Thunderhoof. He ran his hand along the stallion's neck and down its back and said in awe, "Magnificent. Simply magnificent. You have far surpassed my expectations."

"I take it you're pleased," Fargo said drily.

"These animals are superb. I can't thank you enough." Bell offered his hand, and when Fargo took it, shook warmly. "You have done more for me than you can possibly imagine." He glanced at Small Badger and his smile faded. "Who is this?"

Fargo introduced his friend. "The tribe sent him to collect the rest of the money. There were two others but we ran into some trouble."

"Hostiles?" Bell guessed.

Briefly, Fargo told him about the half-breeds.

"You say they were the same three who tried to steal your Ovaro that day Jim Stoddard found you? They must have followed you to Nez Perce country just to get back at you."

"There was more to it than that. They were dead set against you having these Appaloosas. Any idea why?"

"None whatsoever. I've never heard of any Speckled Wolf. I can't begin to guess their motive."

Fargo happened to notice Griff Jackson on the porch. Was it his imagination or did the corners of the foreman's mouth lift in a sly smirk? "We'd like to get our money and be on our way."

"Nonsense," Bell said. "You must be hungry and tired. I insist you accept the hospitality of my home. Bed your Ovaro in the stable and wash up at the bunkhouse and come have supper. It's the least I can do after all you've been through."

"And Small Badger?"

Clarence Bell gave the young Nez Perce a closer scrutiny. "You two became close on the ride here, I take it."

"I've known him longer than that. This is Gray Bear's son. I told you about them at Sweetwater Station."

"Ah. Yes, you did. So when you called him a *friend* you meant exactly that."

Fargo thought Bell's comment was strange. "If he wasn't I wouldn't have said it."

"Well then, he's invited to supper as well."

"Mr. Bell?" Griff Jackson said.

"You heard me. Both of them. Tell the cook to set an extra plate out. It should prove entertaining."

Fargo held out his hand. "I'll take the rest of my money. You also owe Small Badger for the Appaloosas."

The rancher laughed. "Honestly, now. Do you truly expect me to carry that much cash around in my pocket? I'll pay both of you what is due at supper. In the meantime, why don't you tend to your horses and wash up as I suggested? By then it will be almost mealtime."

Fargo reached for the lead rope.

"Leave the Appaloosas. I'd like to admire them a while."

They were halfway to the stable when Small Badger leaned toward Fargo and stressed yet again, "I not like this place."

"No one has taken a shot at you, have they?" Fargo poked fun. "And Bell invited you to supper."

"Yes. But him not want to. I see it in his eyes."

"I'll go by myself then. You can stay with the horses."

Jim Stoddard came out of the stable carrying a bridle. He spotted them and gave Fargo a friendly smile. "You made it in one piece." He looked toward the ranch house. "And you brought the Appaloosas, I see."

"*We* brought them," Fargo amended, and clapped Small Badger on the back.

"That's right. I plumb forgot. Mr. Bell only paid them part of the money."

"He'll pay the rest soon enough," Fargo said.

"You did what no one else could do," Stoddard praised him. "Thanks to you the Circle B will prosper."

"Don't forget your cows."

Stoddard winced as if he had been hit. "The ranch needs more than them. Now that Mr. Bell is the first white man to get his hands on a breeding pair of Appaloosas, he'll have . . ." Stoddard stopped. "Listen to me, running off at the mouth. I have work to do." He touched his hat brim and started to walk off but stopped. "Fargo?" he said quietly.

Fargo looked at him.

"I like you. So consider this a word to the wise. There are more important things in life than money." With that, he jangled off.

"Why him say that?" Small Badger wondered.

"I'll ask him the next time I see him." Fargo entered the stable and found empty stalls for both their horses. The Ovaro went in willingly but when Small Badger tried to coax his Appaloosa, the horse balked. Small Badger pulled on the reins but the Appaloosas refused to be budged.

"Him never do this before."

"Could be he doesn't like being hemmed in," Fargo speculated. The horse wasn't used to four walls and a roof.

"I keep him outside."

Fargo stripped his saddle and saddle blankets and bridle. In a bin were some oats, on a peg the bucket he needed. As he was leaving the stall it occurred to him that Small Badger hadn't come back. He went out, the Henry in the crook of his elbow.

The young warrior and his Appaloosa were gone.

Puzzled, Fargo headed for the ranch house. Laughter brought him to a stop.

He walked to the corner of the stable. From the rear came more gruff glee. He moved faster. Behind the stable was a corral. In it, eleven horses milled about. Past the corral were several punchers. Fargo couldn't see what they were doing but he did see Small Badger's Appaloosa.

". . . you stinking redskin. Get up so I can keep knocking you down until you can't get up anymore."

The tough wore a high-crowned hat and jeans. He had his fists balled and was standing over Small Badger, smugly waiting for him to rise. The other two hands were grinning in sadistic approval.

Fargo gave them no warning. He walked around the corral and over to the cowboy who had hit Small Badger. The man looked up and started to turn and Fargo smashed the Henry's stock against his jaw. Not once but twice, each blow so swift the puncher had no hope of warding them off. As the man fell Fargo pivoted and drove the Henry's barrel into the gut of the second cowboy, doubling him over.

"You son of a bitch!" The third puncher galvanized to life and clawed for his revolver.

Fargo struck him just once and the hand crumpled. Spinning, Fargo slammed the Henry over the head of the man he had slugged in the gut. All three were down. Stepping back, he leveled the rifle in case any of them had some fight left.

Small Badger blinked in amazement. Blood trickled from his mouth and his lower lip was puffy. "Thank you," he said.

Fargo reached down and pulled him to his feet.

"That one hit me."

"He give you a reason?"

"Him say he hate my kind more than anything."

"Another damn Indian hater."

Small Badger gingerly touched his pulped lip. "They see me when I come out. They act nice. They say they have something to show me." He grimaced. "We still go to supper?"

Before Fargo could answer, Griff Jackson came around the corral, his hand on the butt of his Smith and Wesson. "There's going to be hell to pay for this."

17

Fargo spun and trained the Henry on the foreman but Jackson ignored him and walked up to the cowboys. His face red with fury, he kicked each of the unconscious men in the side.

"Damn them to hell."

For a moment Fargo thought Jackson was going to draw and shoot them but the foreman controlled his temper and stepped back.

"I heard the tail end of what the Injun just said. These jackasses shouldn't have done that."

"Friendly hands you've got working for the Circle B," Fargo said.

Jackson's fingers flexed over the Smith and Wesson. "I hadn't gotten to these three yet to tell them you were Mr. Bell's guests. They were acting on their own."

"That's no excuse."

"Look, mister," Jackson said testily, "some people can't stand redskins. They'd as soon shoot an Injun as look at him. Your friend should count himself lucky they didn't do worse."

Fargo indulged in a rare threat. "The next time one of your punchers lays a hand on my friend, they answer to me."

"Do what you have to," Jackson said. "Anyone who doesn't listen to Mr. Bell deserves to be toes up."

Some of Fargo's anger evaporated. "Let's go," he said to Small Badger, and strode off.

"I told you this place bad medicine."

"We'll eat, we'll get our money, and we'll light a shuck, and if we never see the Circle B again, it will be fine by me."

Clarence Bell opened the front door to Fargo's knock. He had changed into a white shirt and dinner jacket. "Mr. Fargo. And your friend. Come in, please. We have time for a drink before supper is served."

"Small Badger," Fargo said to him.

"I beg your pardon?"

"My friend has a name. Use it."

"Is something the matter?"

"Look at his face. Three of your hands were about to stomp him into the dirt."

"What's that? I gave orders that you were to be given special regard," Bell declared. "Who were the men involved? I'll send for my foreman and have him deal with them."

"He already is."

"Well, then. All is well." Bell closed the door and ushered them to a parlor that contained a settee, chairs and a liquor cabinet. He opened the cabinet and took out a bottle. "Only the best. A glass for me and a glass for you, I take it. But what about your . . . sorry, what about Small Badger?"

"I speak the white tongue," the young warrior said.

"Do you, now? How commendable. If more Indians had your initiative there wouldn't be as much blood spilled."

"My what?"

"Your desire to do as whites do. Most Indians couldn't be bothered to learn English."

Fargo broke in with, "That works both ways. Most whites can't be bothered to learn Indian tongues."

Bell removed three glasses from the cabinet. "Why should we? Fifty years from now the white man will control every square foot of land between the Mississippi River and the Pacific Ocean. All the tribes will be on reservations or will have been exterminated."

"What that mean?" Small Badger asked Fargo.

"Wiped out."

"Nimipuu never be wiped out," Small Badger told their host. "Nimipuu strong."

"Arrows and lances are no match for rifles and revolvers," the rancher responded. "But come. I didn't invite you here to talk politics. We'll eat, drink and make merry."

Fargo had to hand it to him. The meal was fine fare. It began with the before-supper drink and then a bowl of soup. Fargo wasn't much of a soup eater but he was famished. He smeared four slices of bread with butter and dipped them in the broth. Next came the main course: thick slabs of juicy beef, potatoes with the skins on, tomatoes and succotash. For dessert there was hot apple pie.

Fargo washed the food down with four cups of steaming-hot coffee. He even added cream and sugar.

Small Badger didn't eat nearly as much. He spooned small portions and only nibbled at his steak.

"You don't like white food?" Clarence Bell asked as the meal was winding down.

"Food fine. I just not eat a lot. Have a long ride tonight."

"It's dangerous to be abroad after sunset. The two of you are welcome to stay in the bunkhouse and leave first thing in the morning."

"Your hands would love that," Fargo said.

"If I say you can sleep in my bunkhouse, you damn well can. I run the Circle B from top to bottom and I don't tolerate dissent."

"What is that?" Small Badger wanted to learn.

"It's where no one gets to do as they want," Fargo translated. "They only get to do as *he* wants."

Bell sat back and swirled the coffee in his china cup. "You make it sound like a bad thing. If you ran your own ranch you would see things differently."

He sipped and delicately set the cup down. "I'm trying to carve order out of chaos, to build a ranch where none has ever existed. It's not bad enough that I must contend with nature's tantrums. I must also deal with hostiles and predators and a host of other problems."

"No one is holding a gun to your head," Fargo said.

"True. I came here of my own free will and I stay because I want to. And I'll do whatever it takes to succeed."

"The Appaloosas should make it easier."

Bell was about to take another sip but stopped and smiled. "Yes. Yes, they will. I'll have the only herd other than the Nez Perce. It should fill my coffers considerably."

"Coffers?" Small Badger said.

"It will make him rich," Fargo explained.

"It not make my people rich."

Clarence Bell laughed. "You're red, for God's sake. Indians don't have a head for business. Not like whites do. Your people keep most of the Appaloosas for yourselves. You only trade or sell them when there is something you need. Me, I plan to let the whole world know. I'll advertise back East. I'll praise the Appaloosa to high heaven. I'll make them out to be the best horse ever bred, and before you know it, everyone in the country will want one. Other breeders, too. But I'll never sell a stallion that isn't gelded. I, and only I, will have Appaloosas to sell. No one else."

"My people have them," Small Badger said.

"Yes, but you're hardly competition." Bell raised the china cup in a salute. "My personal feelings aside, I must thank you for being so reasonable. I'll never forget what your tribe has done for me."

"I tell my people you thank them."

"Ah, yes. Of course. You do that." Bell chuckled. "The irony is too delicious for words."

"Irony?" Fargo said.

"Yes. That it should be Indians, of all people, who have become my salvation. If there is a God he has a wicked sense of humor."

"I'm not sure I savvy."

"Don't you? No, I suppose you haven't figured it out yet. Very well. What better to talk about while we let our food digest. Then we can get to the payment you are due and I can get on with running my ranch." Clarence Bell shifted in his chair and crossed his legs. "The thing is, you see, that I hate Indians with every fiber of my being."

"What?"

"Sorry?" from Small Badger.

"You both heard me right. I *hate* Indians. And no, it's not because my father or my grandfather or my cousin was butchered and scalped. That's the usual reason." Bell smiled. "I hate Indians because they *are* Indians. Or to be more exact, I hate them because they have red skin."

"Hell," Fargo said.

"While I'm being so honest, I'll admit I also hate blacks and Mexicans and the Chinese and anyone else who isn't white."

"You're one of those."

"A bigot, you mean? Yes, I suppose that would be your word for it. Personally, I call it pride in my own race. Pride in being white. An Indian can have pride in being an Indian, can't he? A black can have pride in being black? So why is it wrong for a white man to have pride in being white?"

"Pride is one thing," Fargo said. "Hate is another."

"You're splitting hairs," Bell replied. "If a person has true pride in their race, it stands to reason they won't think highly of any other. It's a matter of breeding. Much like with the Nez Perce and their Appaloosas."

"I not understand," Small Badger said.

"Of course you don't. You're red. Permit me to explain." Bell placed his elbow on his leg and gestured expansively. "People breed just like animals. Some breeds have good traits. Some breeds don't. Your Appaloosas, for example, are famous for being some of the best horses anywhere. And just as there are good and bad breeds of horses, there are good and bad breeds of people."

"All this is leading up to something," Fargo suspected, and moved his hand so it was at the edge of the table above his Colt.

"Assuredly. Be patient. I'll get to the point shortly." Bell sipped coffee. "I mention all this so you will understand what is to follow. You see, not only do I take pride in my race but I act on that pride. How, you wonder. I act on it by killing every redskin, nigger and greaser I catch on the Circle B."

"You son of a bitch."

"Now, now. Hold your temper, Mr. Fargo. I'm not done yet and you will want to hear the rest." Bell paused. "Would you like more coffee? The pot is empty and I know I would."

Fargo didn't answer. Small Badger appeared bewildered.

"This will only take a moment." Bell raised his hand and snapped his fingers as he had done earlier in the meal. The last time, the cook had brought out the pie and set it on the table. But when Bell snapped his finger this time, Griff Jackson and the three punchers who had jumped Small Badger down at the corral entered, each with his revolver out. The foreman pointed his at Fargo. The hammer was already thumbed back.

Fargo started to lower his hand to his Colt the instant he saw them but stopped. He would be dead before he touched it.

"A precaution on my part," Clarence Bell said smugly. "What I am about to say will upset you even more." He motioned. "Mr. Jackson, if you would, kindly relieve Mr. Fargo of his six-shooter and the Indian of his knife."

The three punchers were studies in pure hate. They covered Fargo and Small Badger while Jackson took their weapons, walked around the table, and set them next to Bell.

Bell practically split his face with his smirk. "Now then. Where was I? Oh, yes. I was telling you how much I hate Indians and everyone else in this world who isn't white."

"If you hate them so much," Fargo brought up, "why in hell did you send me to the Nez Perce for Appaloosas?"

"I hate them, not their horses." Bell leaned toward him.

"I need that breeding pair. I need them more than you can imagine. You see, I'm not as wealthy as I claimed. In fact, I am barely making ends meet. It cost much more than I anticipated to get my ranch up and running and the cost of getting my beef to market reduces my profit to next to nothing."

"Starting a ranch this far out was pretty stupid," Fargo remarked to get his dander up.

"Not at all. It was brilliant. So is my solution to the problem. You see, I need something else to sell besides beef. Something that will bring in a lot of money and keep the Circle B afloat. A while back I happened to be at the trading post and saw several Nez Perce and their wonderful mounts. That's when the idea hit me."

There was the answer.

Fargo wanted to kick himself for letting himself be used. But then, how was he to know what Bell was really like?

"Coincidentally enough, that must have been when Speckled Wolf and his two friends overheard me making my plans."

"You knew who they were all along?"

"I was at a table talking with Mr. Jackson. We were near a window. At one point I heard footsteps and looked out and saw Speckled Wolf and the others running off. They must have heard every word I said and decided to stop me. You see, they were aware of how I feel about nonwhites. They had the gall to show up at the house one day asking for work. I explained to them that I would never hire them because they were half red, and that the only reason I would let them leave my ranch alive was because they were half white."

Fargo bowed his head.

"They must have taken it on themselves to try and thwart me. That they were killed by warriors from the very tribe they were trying to help is yet another of life's delightful ironies, wouldn't you agree?"

"You're a sick bastard."

"Sick how? In my head? Oh, please. To my way of thinking, a man like you is the sick one. You've lived with Indians. From what I understand, you've even slept with their women. It's the same as sleeping with dogs. You have no pride in your own race, sir."

Small Badger cleared his throat. "This mean I not get money to take to my people?"

"I couldn't pay you the rest if I wanted to," Clarence Bell said. "I used about all the money I have when I hired Mr. Fargo."

"So you trick us?" Small Badger said.

"From the very start, yes," Bell boasted. "I had to make it seem as if I was rolling in money so Mr. Fargo would be duped into believing I was good for the rest. It worked beautifully, if I do say so myself."

Fargo simmered with fury. If not for the pistols trained on him, he would have been out of his chair and on Bell in a heartbeat.

The rancher stood and smoothed his jacket. "I've done you the courtesy of explaining so you will understand what comes next. You see, Mr. Fargo, I know you have friends in the army, and others. It's conceivable that someone might come nosing around asking about you. Or the Nez Perce might show up in force looking for Small Badger here and the rest of their money. I'll say that I paid you the money due and the two of you rode off and that was the last I ever saw of you. No one will suspect the truth."

"You think of everything, boss," Griff Jackson said.

"That I do. Which is why Mr. Fargo and his red friend must now disappear off the face of the earth."

"Disappear?" Small Badger said.

"Why yes, boy. You're both going to die."

18

Fargo's shoulders throbbed with pain. He had been hanging from a rafter in the stable for the better part of an hour. Twisting, he pried at the knots but they were too tight. He couldn't loosen them.

Small Badger dangled a few feet away. He had not said much since they were hauled from the ranch house and trussed up like calves for the slaughter. Now he raised his head and asked, "Why they not kill us right away?"

"You're complaining?" Fargo commenced to swing his legs back and forth. "Bell has something special planned. I don't know what but we're not sticking around to find out." Fargo swung harder, his boots pressed together, his body rigid.

"What you do?"

"We're getting the hell out of here."

Outside, night had fallen. The puncher left to guard them had muttered something about needing a chaw and had gone out the double doors. He could be back any moment.

Fargo arced his legs at the beam. He couldn't quite reach it. Firming every muscle in his body, he tried again. Yet another swing, and he parted his legs wide and wrapped them around the timber.

"What good that do?" Small Badger wanted to know.

"Keep an eye out." Fargo glanced at the double doors. No sign yet of the cowhand. Bunching his shoulders, he slid the rope, and his hands, toward his boots. It was slow going. He could slide the rope only a few inches at a time. It seemed to take forever but at last his fingers were there. Hiking at his pant leg, he slid his fingers inside his boot and gripped the Arkansas toothpick.

Small Badger grinned. "I forget about knife."

Fargo reversed his grip to cut. The edge was razor sharp but the rope was thick. He had to press hard, which was difficult to do. He bent his wrists to where they hurt like hell.

"Hurry," Small Badger urged.

"What do you think I *am* doing?" Fargo cut and cut until he felt the rope give slightly. His fingers were crucibles of agony.

"I hear someone," Small Badger said.

Fargo heard it, too; whistling, from the direction of the bunkhouse, coming closer. It must be the guard on his way back. He slashed with all his strength. The rope parted and gravity took over. If not for his legs around the beam, he would have dropped headfirst.

The whistler was almost to the stable. Fargo unwrapped his legs, and dropped, flipping in midair so he landed on his feet. Quickly, he ran to Small Badger and cut him down. The young warrior began to say something. Fargo put a finger to his lips and turned toward the entrance. He intended to duck behind one of the doors and stab the puncher when he came in. But the man was already in the doorway, rooted in surprise.

"Run," Fargo said, and shoved Small Badger toward the back. He ran, too.

He dearly wished he could take the Ovaro from the stall and throw on his saddle but the cowboy was clawing for his six-shooter.

Small Badger slowed and glanced back.

Grabbing him by the shoulders, Fargo ducked and pulled Small Badger down just as the revolver went off. Lead sizzled the air above their heads. "Stay low!" he warned, and scuttled like a crab into the shadows.

"Get back here!" the cowhand bellowed.

Fargo slammed into the rear door with his shoulder even as his hand found the latch. He spilled out into the corral and nearly pitched to his knees. Another shot boomed as they ran toward the horses. Fargo figured to climb on one and escape bareback but the horses had been spooked by the ruckus and shied away.

"Him after us," Small Badger warned.

The jingle of spurs was ominously loud.

Fargo pushed Small Badger toward the rails. "Climb over. I'll be right behind you." He looked around for a weapon. A rock, a whip, a rope, anything. There was none to be had.

Small Badger was clambering up. He gained the top and lowered his arm to help. "Grab me."

"No need." Taking two long strides, Fargo bounded high enough to catch hold of the top rail and pull himself up and over. Another shot cracked as he dropped to the other side.

"What now, Iron Will?"

"We run like hell."

Fargo flew for all he was worth. He had always been fleet of foot and he proved it again now by springing ahead of his young friend. Together they fled into the dark with no goal in mind other than to save their hides.

The puncher was hollering up a storm.

"Him call others."

"Keep running."

A glance at the sky told Fargo they were running east. They were past the outhouses, on open ground. He tried not to think of what might happen should they step into a hole or a rain-worn rut.

Another shot split the night but the puncher was firing blind. Other men were shouting back and forth. From the house came an angry shout that sounded like Griff Jackson.

"My side hurt where man kick me," Small Badger said between puffs.

"You'll hurt a lot worse if they get their hands on you again," Fargo said to coax him to greater speed. He glanced back.

The horses in the corral were prancing and whinnying. Men moved among them, seeking to throw saddles on. Other punchers were circling around the corral and giving chase on foot.

"They after us."

"Keep running."

They had covered several hundred yards when the first rider burst out of the corral gate and came galloping after them. A second and a third were hard on his hooves.

Grabbing Small Badger, Fargo veered toward a dark patch to their left. The patch broadened into a dry wash. Hurtling down, Fargo flattened and pulled the young warrior down beside him. Small Badger was breathing heavily and had a hand pressed to his ribs.

"I hurt worse."

"Lie still. It will pass." Fargo crawled to the top and risked a peek.

Four riders had spread out and were coming in their general direction.

The four began yelling back and forth.

"Any sign of them?"

"Not here."

"Nothing this way."

"The big sugar says that no matter what, we can't let them get away."

"Do we shoot to kill?"

"You damn sure do."

Fargo slid down and plucked at Small Badger's sleeve. "Stay close." He bent and ran along the bottom and had gone a short way when he realized Small Badger hadn't moved. Fargo hurried back. "What in blazes are you waiting for?"

Torment contorted Small Badger's face. "Where man kick me is much hurt. I think maybe he break rib bone."

"Stay put, then." Fargo scrambled to the top again. One of the riders, standing tall in the stirrups and looking right and left, was nearing the wash. Fargo ducked down. His hand brushed an object that rolled and he clutched it before it could clatter and give him away. It was a rock about the size of a hen's egg. Hefting it, he listened to the approaching thud of hooves and when the horse was right on top of him he reared up.

The cowboy swore in surprise and stabbed for his six-gun.

Fargo threw the rock. It caught the man full in the face and he caterwauled and reeled in the saddle. Fargo helped him along by springing, seizing a leg, and wrenching. The puncher fell hard on his shoulder and head and didn't move.

From across the way came a shout. "Macky? Was that you? What's going on over there?"

Fargo snagged the mount's reins. He groped at the fallen puncher's holster but it was empty. The revolver had fallen out. As much as Fargo wanted to look for it, there was no time. Vaulting up, he reined into the wash.

Small Badger was on his feet. He didn't need to be told what to do; he raised an arm over his head.

Bending, Fargo gripped and swung Small Badger up behind him. A jab of his spurs and they were off, flying along the ravine as if their mount was lighter than air. From above and behind rose yells of alarm.

Fargo swept around a bend and then another—and the wash ended.

Without slowing, he galloped up the side and was out in the open. He lashed the reins as men clamored and guns boomed. Hornets buzzed dangerously near.

"Keep your head down," he urged, and flew.

Riding in the dark was always a perilous proposition. It didn't help that Fargo was unfamiliar with the terrain and wasn't riding his own horse. He reined sharply to avoid a boulder, reined again to sweep around a mound that might be a prairie dog burrow.

"Stop them, damn it!"

That sounded like Griff Jackson. Fargo shifted and noticed something jutting from the saddle scabbard. He jerked it free, and grinned. Fate had granted him a Spencer rifle to fight back with. Jamming it to his shoulder, he yelled, "Duck!" to Small Badger, and twisted around. He couldn't fix a bead for all the up-and-down movement of the horse but he fired anyway.

"He's got a gun!" someone bawled.

To a man, his pursuers slowed.

Fargo resorted anew to his spurs. "Hang on tight." He rode on, a long, hard, brutal ride, never once stopping until eventually he looked back and no one was there. He slowed to a walk. The only hoofbeats he heard were those of his mount. "I think we did it." Small Badger didn't answer.

"Didn't you hear me? We got away." Fargo chuckled and slid the Spencer into the scabbard. "Small Badger?"

The young warrior groaned.

Fargo shifted. Small Badger's chin was on his chest and his arms were starting to droop. Clutching him to keep him from sliding off, Fargo drew rein. His hand where it touched Small Badger's shirt became wet.

"No," Fargo said, and quickly dismounted. Carefully, he lowered Small Badger to the grass and placed him on his back. His other hand became wet.

Dreading what he would find, Fargo hiked his friend's shirt. He couldn't find a wound anywhere on the front, not on the chest or the belly or even the shoulder. Puzzled, Fargo rolled him partway over, and grimaced. A slug had caught Small Badger between the shoulder blades. It must still be in his body because there was no exit wound.

Fargo gently eased Small Badger down. He was about to stand and see if there was a canteen on the horse when Small Badger's eyes fluttered open and he sucked in a long breath.

"Iron Will?"

"I'm here." Fargo grasped his hand. "Why didn't you tell me you were shot?"

"You would stop. Maybe be shot too."

"You kept quiet for my sake?" Fargo coughed to get rid of a constriction in his throat. "Damn it. You shouldn't have."

"You be mad at me?"

"No," Fargo said more gruffly than he intended.

"Then why you sound mad?"

Fargo changed the subject. "The lead is still inside you. I'll get a fire going and try to dig it out."

"Badmen will see fire."

"Let them." Fargo started to rise but Small Badger grasped his wrist.

"No. Please. No need."

"I might be able to save you," Fargo tried to pull loose but Small Badger held firm. "Let go, damn it."

"I sorry," Small Badger said.

"For what?"

"I not can help you fight. They are many and you are one. Do smart thing and ride far away." Small Badger coughed and dark stains appeared at the corners of his mouth.

"God, no."

"I not expect rancher to hate so much. I think him must be good man because he send you."

Fargo looked away for a moment and clenched his fists so tight his fingernails dug into his palms. "Stop talking and lie still. I'll cut out the slug and bandage you and in a couple of weeks you'll be as good as can be."

"Tell Father I say it not your fault. Tell him how rancher tricked you. Tell him I say you friend to Nimipuu."

"Don't do this," Fargo said.

"No do what?"

"Don't die on me."

"You always good friend, Iron Will. I proud ride with you." Small Badger smiled.

"And I'm proud to call you my pard."

"Iron Will?"

"Save your breath, damn it."

"I feel funny in head."

"I'm digging that bullet out whether you want me to or not." Fargo drew the Arkansas toothpick and tested the edge on his thumb. He began to roll Small Badger onto his side and realized Small Badger wasn't breathing. He felt for a pulse, and then quaked as if to a cold wind. For a long while he knelt there, unmoving. Then he slowly stood and turned toward the Circle B.

"I'm coming for you, you sons of bitches."

19

The Circle B hands were still hunting for them.

Fargo spotted the first puncher before the man spotted him. He reined up and dismounted and let the reins dangle. Stepping around behind the horse, he crouched.

The cowboy came on slowly, warily, his revolver out, ready to shoot.

He saw the horse and reined toward it. When he saw the saddle was empty he glanced every which way and then drew rein a few yards out. Aloud he said, "Where the hell did they get to?"

Fargo tensed for his rush.

The cowboy turned his head and shouted, "Over here! I found their horse but there's no sign of them!"

The instant the man turned, Fargo was up and around his mount. He thrust the Spencer against the puncher's chest and the startled cowboy looked down and bleated in fear.

"No!"

"Yes," Fargo said, and shot him. One was all it took. The man slumped to the ground and Fargo grabbed the reins so the horse wouldn't run off. He heard others galloping toward him.

Fargo led the second animal over to the one he had been riding. He moved behind his horse and dropped flat.

This time there were two punchers. They approached as cautiously as the first man. One of them spotted the prone form and they stopped and climbed down. Six-shooters at their sides, they advanced as if walking on eggshells. One knelt next to the body.

"It's Sam. He's dead."

"Where did they get to?" the other asked.

"They must have run off."

"And left these horses? That doesn't make no sense."

They looked about, scouring the benighted plain.

In a crouch Fargo moved between the two horses. When the two cowboys came up to take the reins he stepped out and shot the man on the right in the head and spun and rammed the Henry against the other's temple. Both folded. He relieved the second man of a Colt, slid it into his holster, and straightened.

Fargo waited. He was in no hurry. To go charging off was suicide. He would do it smart and work his way to the top.

After a while the second cowboy groaned. His hat had fallen off and when he opened his eyes he groped the ground for it. He then saw Fargo standing over him. "You."

"Me." Fargo pointed the Spencer at his face.

"Don't shoot, mister! Please!"

"What's your name?"

"Walker. Ira Walker. You have no call to kill me. I wasn't one of those who beat on the redskin."

"How do you feel about them?"

"How do I feel about who?"

"Indians. Do you hate them as much as your boss does? As much as those three who hurt my friend?"

"I don't hate anybody. I punch cows, is all, and Mr. Bell pays well. Or did until he started having money trouble."

"You want me to let you live."

"God, yes."

"You were hunting me."

"I was in the bunkhouse. I heard a ruckus. They said you stole a horse and we all came after you."

Fargo took a step back and swung the Spencer up so the barrel was on his shoulder. "I have a job for you, Ira Walker."

"How's that again?"

144

"Get on your horse and ride back to the ranch. Tell your friends to light a shuck while they can."

"Are you loco? Mr. Bell has thirty hands working for him. Why should they run from just one hombre?"

"It's twenty-eight now," Fargo said, "and a lot of them are out on the range tending cattle. I only counted nine when I rode up today. That leaves seven counting you." Fargo paused. "Come to think of it, you only need to tell one man he can go."

"You're confusing the hell out of me."

"Do you know Jim Stoddard?"

"Of course."

"He's the one. The rest are dead. They just don't know it yet."

"Says you."

"On your feet."

Ira Walker slowly sat up. "I'll tell Stoddard. I'll also tell Mr. Bell you're out for blood."

"You do that. Get going."

Walker glanced at the two dead punchers. "Those were good men you killed."

"Someone shot my friend in the back. It could have been one of them." Fargo pointed the Henry. "It could have been you."

Walker held his hands out. "Hold on. I haven't fired a shot all night." He sidled toward his horse. "If you were smart you'd get out while you can. You can't kill all of us. Not you alone you can't."

"Planning to stay and fight?"

"Hell, no. I'm no gun hand. My life is cows and only cows. After I find Stoddard and tell Mr. Bell, I'm collecting my plunder from the bunkhouse and fanning the breeze for Texas. I haven't seen my ma in a spell and I miss her cooking."

"If you're lying, you'll die."

Walker raised a boot to the stirrup. "You're awful sure of yourself."

"You're good with cows, you say."

"Damn good. I worked on two ranches in Texas before I drifted up this way."

"I'm good at tracking and scouting and living off the land, and one other thing."

Walker bobbed his head. "I savvy." He slowly forked leather and slowly raised the reins. "Anything else?"

"Tell Clarence Bell I'm saving him for last. Tell him it won't be quick or easy. He can run if he wants but I'll find him."

"Mister, you have some thick bark on you."

"Go."

"What about my six-gun?"

Fargo raised the Spencer to his shoulder.

"All right. All right. I'm leaving. Damn, you are as curly a wolf as I ever hope to meet."

Fargo stood until the thud of hooves faded. Then he took a Smith and Wesson revolver from the second man he had shot and tucked it under his belt. He climbed on the horse he had been using, snagged the reins to the other animal, and returned to where he had left Small Badger. He untied the bedroll on his horse, spread out the blankets, placed Small Badger on top of them, and rolled his friend up. After tying the blanket at both ends, he draped the body over the second horse and secured it with rope.

Fargo headed for the Circle B. He encountered no one along the way and eventually the lights of the ranch flared in the distance. A stand of cottonwoods materialized out of the murky gloom and he rode in and tied the second horse. He drew the Colt and the Smith and Wesson and made sure each had six pills in the wheel. "I reckon I'm ready," he said to the empty air.

Fargo made for the lights. Bell and the punchers would be waiting for him. They would set an ambush and expect him to ride into it.

Fargo reined wide to the south, searching. He figured there

would be cattle close by and he was right. He discovered a herd of forty head or so, bedded down. He looked for a night guard but there was none.

All it took to stampede them was three shots into the ground and a war whoop a Comanche would be proud of. Mooing and lowing, they heaved to their feet and lumbered into motion. The trick was to keep them pointed toward the buildings.

Coughing from the choking cloud of dust they raised, Fargo rode hard on their tails. He reloaded, never easy on a moving horse.

A figure appeared at a second-floor window in the ranch house. Clarence Bell had heard the din and was looking out.

Fargo went on swallowing dust until the cows were a hundred yards out. Then he broke off and galloped in a loop that brought him up on the other side of the ranch house just as the herd stampeded among the buildings.

Drawing rein, Fargo alighted. He ran to the back door and tried the latch.

The door opened silently on well-oiled hinges. A short hallway brought him to a flight of polished oak steps. He went up three at a stride and down the hall to the door to the room where he had seen Bell. He didn't bother with the latch. He kicked the door in and dived for the floor with his Colt extended.

The room was empty.

Fargo checked under the bed and in the closet. No one. But he *had* seen Bell at the window. He glanced out. The pane above him shattered, raining sharp shards. The boom of a rifle explained why.

Fargo ducked and darted to the hall and over to the steps. He started down but stopped at the beat of heavy boots. Two men, at least. He retreated into the room he had just vacated and hunkered behind the door. The crack between the door and the jamb was wide enough that he could see the top of the stairs.

A head appeared. A grizzled cowboy, one of the three who had jumped Small Badger at the corral.

Fargo stayed where he was.

The head disappeared and there was whispering. Tucked at the knees, his six-gun in front of him, the cowboy climbed the last few steps. Behind him came another. They edged forward, peering into each room.

Fargo filled his left hand with the Smith and Wesson. He marked each step and when they were near he threw himself around the door in a headlong dive. The first cowboy snapped off a shot but was too hasty. Fargo fired the Colt into the first man and the Smith and Wesson into the second. Both fell, the first lifeless, the other alive enough to try to take aim. Fargo pointed both revolvers at him and stroked both triggers.

The house went quiet.

Fargo rose. There were no outcries. No one came running to help. He crept to the stairs, listened, and then went down them with his back to the wall. He made for the back door but abruptly reversed and went to the dining room.

They were still there, his Colt and the Henry, lying on the table where Clarence Bell had placed them when Griff Jackson and the others disarmed him. He set down the revolvers he had taken from the cowboys and reclaimed his own weapons.

Fargo felt whole again. He went to the front of the house and stood to one side of the front door. With a quick flip of the latch he opened it and shoved it wide.

Instantly, two rifles banged and lead bit into the wood. Splinters went flying.

Fargo moved to a window. Removing his hat, he put his eye to the edge of the glass. A lantern lit the entry to the stable and two of the bunkhouse windows were aglow. Otherwise the buildings showed no signs of life.

Then, from somewhere in the darkness, a shout.

"Kline, can you hear me in there? Did you get him or not?"

Fargo cupped a hand to his mouth. "Not."

Out in the dark, Clarence Bell swore. "Fargo, you bastard. We have you surrounded. Give up and I'll make it quick."

"I'm just getting started."

"You're a damn fool. But what else should I expect from an Indian lover? If you had any brains you'd think the same as me."

"You have any brothers and sisters?"

"What kind of question is that? I have a sister. Why do you ask?"

"She anything like you?"

"Hell, no. She lives down in Santa Fe with some Mexican she married. She wrote me once asking me to visit but I'd as soon shoot her as be under the same roof with a Mex."

Jamming his hat back on, Fargo went to a corner table. On it was a lit lamp decorated with red flowers.

"Didn't you hear me? What do you aim to accomplish? One man against all of us?"

Fargo picked up the lamp and hefted it. He carried it over near the window and held it out so Bell and whoever else was out there could see it.

"What's that?" Bell yelled.

"A lamp."

"I can see that, damn it. Why are you holding it? So we won't shoot? Because if we do the lamp might break and set my house on fire?"

"Shoot all you want. It won't make a difference."

"You're loco, do you know that? You can't possibly get away."

"You have it backward."

"What?"

"Small Badger is dead."

"So? What do I care?"

"You will."

"I told you. I hate redskins. There's a saying I'm fond of that sums up my sentiments. Maybe you've heard of it." Clarence Bell paused. "The only good Indian is a dead Indian."

Someone else—it sounded like Griff Jackson—laughed.

"That's telling him, boss."

"There's an expression I'm fond of, too," Fargo responded, and raised the lamp over his head.

"What might that be?" Bell shouted.

"An eye for an eye." Fargo turned and dashed the lamp to the floor.

20

A sheet of flame spurted.

Fargo had thrown the lamp near the curtains and fire leaped up them to the ceiling with a loud *whoosh*. Whirling, he ran into the next room, grabbed another lamp off a stand, and threw it. It smashed into shards and fragments and flame once again spread with astounding rapidity, flowing up the walls and across the ceiling like a thing alive.

From outside came a mixed cry of rage and horror.

Fargo ran to the kitchen. Next to the stove was a woodbin. He smiled as he hoisted another lamp and sent it crashing down. Darting past the fireball, he reached the back door and flung it open.

Ira Walker was ten feet away, a rifle leveled.

They both fired at the same split second. Fargo felt a tug on his sleeve even as Walker was punched backward. Walker looked down at himself, at a stain on his shirt, and cried out, "God in heaven, no!" He took a step and pitched onto his side.

Fargo checked right and left and bounded into the darkness. He expected to be shot at but wasn't. When he had gone about fifty yards he stopped and hunkered.

Red and orange tongues of fire were engulfing the house. It was astounding how quickly the fires he caused swelled into an inferno. Several men were out in front and Clarence Bell was bellowing something about trying to put the fire out but he was deluding himself. A hundred hands with a hundred water buckets would be pressed to stop it now.

Fargo rose and circled. His next stop was the bunkhouse. No one was there. Only two lamps were lit but they were enough. He broke one over a bunk and the other he hurled against a wall. Without waiting to see the effect, he raced out the back door and around to the stable.

Up at the house, Clarence Bell and Griff Jackson and others were mesmerized by the conflagration. Bell broke the spell and ran toward the front porch only to be grabbed and held back by his foreman.

The horses in the stable were agitated. They smelled the smoke and heard the commotion and were stamping and nickering.

Fargo brought the Ovaro out and threw on his saddle blanket and saddle. He shoved the Henry into the scabbard, slipped the bridle on, and led the stallion out the back.

The horses in the corral were milling anxiously about.

Fargo tied the Ovaro to a rail, opened the gate, and flapped his arms. Every horse bolted. Hurrying into the stable, he brought each animal out of its stall, pointed it down the aisle, and gave it a slap on the rump. He saved Thunderhoof and the mare for last. Throwing a rope over them, he took them out and tied them next to the Ovaro.

All that was left was to set the stable on fire.

Fargo went back in but no sooner had he stepped over the threshold than a gun hammer clicked and a man stepped out of a stall.

"I wish you hadn't come back," Jim Stoddard said, his cheek pressed to the stock of a rifle.

"You can leave," Fargo told him.

Stoddard raised his head. "I tried to warn you. I didn't want it to come to this but now it has and you leave me no choice."

"You're siding with Bell?"

"What else did you expect? You asked me once if I ride for the brand and I told you I do."

"The man you ride for is a bigot and a bastard and better off dead."

"Who are you to judge? He's always treated me decent. Sure, he's not fond of Injuns, but who is? I'd as soon they were all breathing dirt."

"Hell," Fargo said.

"Don't look at me like that. I lost an uncle and an aunt to the Comanches. I was only ten but I remember it as clear as can be." Stoddard frowned. "They cut out my uncle's tongue and chopped off his ears and did things to my aunt that I can't talk about to this day."

"My friend never hurt anyone you know."

"No, he didn't. I'd be sorry he's dead if he hadn't of been red." Stoddard tilted his head to listen. Someone was yelling but the words were difficult to make out.

"It doesn't have to be like this," Fargo tried one last time.

"Just stand there. I won't shoot you unless you make me but Mr. Bell needs to know I've caught you." Stoddard shifted and opened his mouth to shout.

Fargo sidestepped, drawing as he moved. The rifle banged and lead bit into the back wall. Fargo's hand seemed to have a mind of its own—it flashed to his holster and out swept the Colt, his thumb curling the hammer as he cleared leather. He fired just once.

Impaled, Jim Stoddard rose onto the tips of his toes and gaped in disbelief.

He took a faltering step, cried out, and died.

At the front of the stable a six-shooter cracked.

Fargo spun and bolted out and was over to the Ovaro and in the saddle and out the gate with Thunderhoof and the mare hard behind him before a silhouette filled the doorway. Again the revolver cracked but he was bent low and heard the slug buzz over his head.

He rode far enough that the Appaloosas wouldn't take a stray bullet.

Taking a picket pin from his saddlebags, he made sure that Thunderhoof and the mare wouldn't stray off.

The house was fully engulfed. Sheets of flame jumped high into the night sky, the wood spitting and hissing like a tormented cat. Only about half of the bunkhouse had burned but the flames were crawling across the roof.

Fargo jogged back. He rounded the corral and stopped at the rear door.

The cowboy who had shot at him was at the front. Two men were approaching from the house, the glow lighting them as bright as day; it was Clarence Bell and Griff Jackson.

The foreman stared at the burning bunkhouse and then hollered at the cowboy in the stable, "Where are those damn horses?"

"They're all gone!"

Fargo went around the corner and along the outside wall.

Clarence Bell looked ready to burst a blood vessel. He was gesturing and swearing and railing at Jackson and Hank and one other man, blaming them for what he had brought down on their heads.

With a tremendous crash a roof timber in the house buckled, taking a third of the roof with it. The flames leaped higher than ever. From out of them flew hundreds of tiny fireflies, rising on the currents.

The four men out front came toward the stable. Bell shook a fist and blistered the air with oaths. Griff Jackson was a mad bull without anyone to gore. The two punchers appeared bewildered by it all.

Fargo stepped past the corner. They didn't notice him at first. Not until he coughed.

Hank pointed and blurted, "It's him! It's Fargo!"

All of them turned. Griff Jackson's hand poised over his Smith and Wesson but he didn't draw. He glanced at his employer.

Clarence Bell was a mouse enraged. He shook a bony fist and called out.

"You dare!"

"Any last words?"

Bell took a step, his face so red it was a wonder he didn't have blood coming out of his eyes and nose. "You arrogant son of a bitch."

"Looked in a mirror lately?"

The rancher gestured at the house and then at the bunkhouse. "My ranch is everything to me and you are doing your best to destroy it. I want you dead so much I can taste it."

"I'm flattered." Fargo was watching Griff Jackson and Hank and the other cowboy. They were coiled to explode the instant their boss gave the word.

"I had it all worked out. You were to bring me the Appaloosas and I would become the only white Appaloosa breeder on the continent." Bell seemed to be talking more to himself than to Fargo. "I'd charge more than the Arabs do for their Arabians. Between the Appaloosas and my cows I would become rich. More money than I ever dreamed of."

"This was all about greed?"

Bell's head snapped up. "What else is there besides money? Wealth is all that matters. With it you are a prince. You can have anything you want. Without it you're nothing."

"Some people think there's more to life."

"Simpletons. Those who don't have money always look down their noses at those who do. They are fools, and worse. Secretly, they envy men like me. Men who take what they want and have no qualms about how they take it."

"Says the gent who cheated me and the Nez Perce and is to blame for the death of my friend."

"You keep harping on that. He was an *Indian*, for God's sake. A gnat. A worthless husk of red skin. How many centuries have his kind had this land and what have they done with it? Nothing. They live in tents made of animal hide and go around with bows and arrows. Compare that to what we've done. The world will be no worse off without them."

Fargo had listened to enough. He set himself. The time had come to end it.

"All this gab of yours about wealth and worthless. This isn't about any of that. This is about you and me and here and now."

"I'm not armed," Bell said.

"Neither was Small Badger when your men shot him in the back."

Hank was shifting his weight from one leg to the other and the fingers of his gun hand were twitching. Fargo had pegged him as the one to break, and now Hank took a step and growled, "Enough, damn it. Let's get this over with. I owe this bastard for the knot on my head."

Griff Jackson took a step. "We do it together. The three of us at the same time. He might be as good as they say but he can't get all three of us. Not all three he can't."

"Who wants to be first?" Fargo taunted.

"Me," Hank said, and drew. He jerked his six-shooter cleanly but it was only half out when Fargo's Colt boomed and Hank dived out of the way.

Griff Jackson was quicker. He drew and fired only a heart-beat slower than Fargo and the only reason he missed was that Fargo was in motion, throwing himself past the corner of the stable.

Fargo had stood next to it on purpose. He glanced out and lead smacked the edge, nearly taking his eye out. Jackson and the other cowboy were backing into the stable, covering Bell.

Fargo turned and ran to the rear. He climbed over the rails into the corral and edged to the back door. Crouching, he peered in.

A lantern lit the front of the stable. The back was in shadow.

Bell and his foreman and hands were nowhere to be seen.

Fargo glided in and over toward the first stall. As he cleared the doorway a revolver spoke. He answered, and then he had the stall between him and them.

He began to replace the two cartridges.

From somewhere at the front of the stable came a mocking laugh. "I just realized, scout. After we kill you I'll find the Appaloosas and take them to Denver. I have a friend there. He'll let me keep them on his ranch. I'll lie low until I'm sure the Nez Perce aren't looking for me." He laughed again. "I can still achieve my dream."

Fargo was tired of Bell's constant jabber. He cocked the Colt and poked his head past the stall and nearly had his hat blown off.

Now it was Hank who laughed. "Show yourself again, mister. I won't miss a second time."

Fargo took a couple of steps back, then launched himself up and over into the next stall. Someone fired and the wood resounded to a loud thump. He landed on his shoulder and rolled up onto his knees.

"Stay calm, men," Clarence Bell advised them. "So long as we keep our wits about us, we'll come out on top."

"Wits, hell," Hank said. "All I want is a clear shot."

"You do as Mr. Bell tells you," Griff Jackson said. "Or by God you'll answer to me."

They were careless, this bunch. Fargo now had a good idea where the three of them were. The only one he was unsure about was the other cowboy. He felt along the bottom of the stall for something to throw but all that was there was straw.

"Yes, the more I think about it, the more I like the idea of Denver," Clarence Bell prattled. "The Nez Perce might come here in force once the chief's son doesn't return. I can't fight an entire tribe."

Across the aisle something moved. Fargo threw himself flat as flame stabbed the dark. He replied, once, twice, three times, and a figure reared clutching its chest, and toppled.

Fargo reloaded.

"Did you get him, Myers?" Bell called out.

"I think Myers is dead," Hank said.

Fargo crawled around the stall and into the next. He raised high enough to see over. Several stalls down a head appeared. He snapped off a shot and was rewarded with a shriek and the crash of a body.

"Hank?" Bell shouted.

"Better be quiet, sir," Jackson warned. "There's just the two of us now."

Fargo darted across the aisle. Farther down the foreman burst from a stall, fanning the Remington. Fargo fanned the Colt. His shoulder stung, and then Griff Jackson was doubled over and firing into the dirt. Fargo fired again and Jackson pitched onto his face and was still.

Fargo had only one cartridge left in the cylinder. He moved down the center aisle and from the ink under the hayloft charged Clarence Bell holding a pitchfork aloft. Fargo let him get so close that Bell grinned, thinking he had him. Then Fargo shot him in the mouth.

Burning the stable down was easy.

Burying Small Badger was hard.

Fargo stood over the grave and said simply, "I'm sorry."

Ten days later Gray Bear stepped out of his lodge at the blush of dawn to find Fargo waiting. Fargo handed him the lead rope to Thunderhoof and the mare and gave him all the money.

Gray Bear looked at him questioningly.

Fargo told him in sign. The hurt and the sorrow that came into the stricken father's eyes tore at his insides. He climbed on the Ovaro and rode from the village.

Gray Bear didn't try to stop him.

Fargo brought the stallion to a gallop. Clarence Bell had been right about one thing. Denver was the place to go. It had enough saloons and bawdy houses that he could stay drunk for a month.

LOOKING FORWARD!
The following is the opening section of the next novel in the exciting *Trailsman* series from Signet:

THE TRAILSMAN #343
TEXAS HELLIONS

Texas, 1860—amid the dust and the fury rides the Trailsman . . .

Skye Fargo first saw the three men when he came out of the Dallas House. They were coming down the street, two white men and a black man, dressed in clothes that would cost most people a year's wages. The black man towered over his companions by a good foot and a half and had a body half as wide as a buckboard. They walked past him and went into the hotel and he bent his boots to the nearest saloon, a watering hole with a sign out front that read BULL BY THE HORNS. Grinning, Fargo went in.

The barkeep was heavyset and bald and showed yellow teeth when he smiled.

"What will it be, mister?"

Fargo took out his poke and opened it. The pitiful few coins he had left brought a frown. He would love a bottle and a night of poker and a warm dove on his lap but that was for those who had money to spare and he sure as hell didn't.

"One drink will have to do."

The bartender poured two-fingers' worth and slid the glass across. "If you are looking for work there's plenty to be had. Dallas is growing like a weed."

"Sure is," Fargo agreed. As frontier towns went, Dallas was downright prosperous. "I saw some men marching in the street earlier," he mentioned.

"That would be the militia. All this talk of secession has everyone worked up. Some think it will be war. What do you think?"

Fargo sipped and sighed as the coffin varnish burned his gullet. "I don't hardly give a damn."

"You haven't picked a side? Down here if you're not for the South you could be tarred and feathered."

"I would like to see someone try." Fargo took another slow slip.

"Bold talk," the barkeep said.

Fargo looked at him. The man blinked, then coughed as if he had something in his throat.

"I didn't mean anything by it. Just making talk, is all."

"I like to drink in peace."

The bartender raised his hands, palms out, and showed his yellow teeth again. "Sure thing." He started to turn, then stopped. "Looks to me like you won't get the chance, though."

Fargo shifted toward the batwings.

The three men he had seen outside the hotel were coming toward him, the two whites in the lead. The wide brims of their hats shadowed their faces and their eyes. The youngest, who wasn't much over twenty and had a thin mustache and no chin to speak of, stopped and said, "You're that scout, aren't you?"

Fargo switched the glass to his left hand and leaned his left elbow on the bar. He lowered his right hand until it brushed his Colt. "Which scout would that be?"

"What do you mean which?"

"There are plenty to go around," Fargo said. "There's Jim Bridger. There's Kit Carson. There's Walker and Colter and others. Which scout did you have in mind?"

The young man glanced at his companion, who also had a thin mustache but could boast a fair chin, and then frowned. "Are you poking fun? You know damn well who I mean. Skye Fargo. The man my pa sent for."

"You would be?"

"Emery Broxton. This here is my brother, Thad. Pa sent us to fetch you to the house."

"Your friend there?" Fargo asked, with a nod at the black.

Emery glanced over his shoulder, and snorted. "Friend? Hell, that's just one of our slaves. We call him Chaku. He comes from Africa. He's nothing."

"Looks like something to me," Fargo said.

"Now I know you must be poking fun. Since when do blacks matter? And how did we get on this, anyhow? Come along. We shouldn't keep Pa waiting."

"I'm not done with my drink yet." Fargo had only a sip left but he could make it two sips if he tried.

"Hell. Finish and we can be on our way."

"They say patience is a virtue."

Emery fidgeted. "You sure as hell are trying mine. All you've done is prick at me, and for no reason."

"I always have a reason," Fargo said. He sipped and had enough left for one more.

Thad chose that moment to say, "We're getting off on the wrong foot, here. My pa sent for you because we need you. We need you bad."

Emery nodded. "Folks say you are the best scout around. Better than Bridger and Carson and . . ." He paused. "Who else was it you said? Walker and some other fellow?"

"If it's the best you want then you want Bridger," Fargo said. "He's been around longer and knows more than me. Carson would be second best. Walker knows California better and there's a mountain man knows every tree in the central Rockies but I've been more places than both of them so we're about tied for third best."

"You're poking fun again, aren't you?"

"Only saying how things are." Fargo savored his last sip. He set the glass down and addressed the black. "What part of Africa?"

Emery made a sound like a goose being strangled. "What the hell are you talking to him for? Didn't you hear me? He's a slave, for God's sake. It's us you have dealings with."

"Please, Mr. Fargo," Thad said diplomatically. "Let us take you to our pa. He'll explain everything."

Emery said, "I'm not so sure sending for you was a good notion. I think you just did that to get my goat."

"You're not as dumb as you look," Fargo replied.

A red tinge crept from Emery's collar to his brow. He balled his fists and took a step. "I won't be insulted."

"Then you shouldn't open your mouth."

Emery swore and swung.

For Fargo it was like dodging molasses. He sidestepped and drove his left fist into the younger Broxton's gut. Not with all his strength but hard enough that Emery staggered back and lost his balance and would have fallen if Chaku hadn't caught him.

"Here now! Enough of that," Thad hollered.

Emery wrenched free of Chaku and straightened, snarling, "Let go, damn you. I don't need no darky helping me." He raised his fists and advanced but Thad stepped in front of him.

"No."

"Out of the way. You saw what he did. I'll beat him black and blue and kick his ribs in."

"Look at him," Thad said.

"What?"

Thad gripped his brother by the shoulder and pointed at Fargo. "Look at him, damn you. *Really* look at him."

Emery did, and some of the red faded.

"You have to able to tell when a man is dangerous and when he's not," Thad said. "This one is as dangerous as they come. You try him and he'll kill you, little brother, and he will do it as slick as you please."

Fargo smiled at Thad. "I reckon you got all the brains."

Thad started to laugh but choked it off and said to Emery, "Listen to me. Forget it. We need him. Whether he is first best or second best or third best is not the issue. He can do it where we can't."

"He made me out to be a fool."

"We can't afford one of your tantrums," Thad said. "Think of Adam and Evie. Think of how much they mean to us."

"She has hair like corn silk."

"Damn it." Thad gripped his brother by the shirt. "Do you want me to tell Pa? Do you honestly want him mad at you?"

"No."

"Then it's over." Thad turned to Fargo. "I'm sorry. He's young and headstrong. And you *did* prod him."

"A little," Fargo conceded.

"If you would be so kind, we'd like to escort you to our home. It's out the south road a ways. We can be there by supper if we leave now."

"I could stand to fill my belly." Fargo let them go out ahead of him. He nodded at Chaku as the big black went to follow the brothers and Chaku gave him a peculiar look. Fargo caught up and remarked, "You don't say much, do you?"

Chaku didn't say anything.

"Is it that you don't speak the white tongue all that well?"

"I speak it good enough."

Fargo chuckled. "That you do." He offered his hand. "Pleased to make your acquaintance."

Chaku stared at Fargo's hand and then at Fargo. "Why you talk to me? Why you treat me like this?"

"Like what?"

"Like you give any kind of damn. I am no one to you. So why you be so friendly?"

"Mother's milk," Fargo said.

"I had mother. I not friendly as you."

"You have cause not to be. You were taken from your land and dragged over here. I'd like to hear about that sometime."

"Why?"

"I was born curious."

"You have big nose, white man. But I do not talk on my past."

"Never?"

"Ever."

Emery and Thad were making for the stable. Emery abruptly stopped and turned and put his hands on his hips. "What the hell is the matter with you? Why are you talking to a slave?"

"There are days when I talk to my horse," Fargo said.

"Damn, you are peculiar. He's nothing. Get that through your noggin. It's us you should be talking to. We're the ones who are hiring you."

"Not yet you haven't," Fargo reminded him. "And it's your pa who sent for me."

"Quit squabbling," Thad snapped at Emery. "The sooner we get there, the sooner he can be on his way."

Emery muttered and walked on.

"I sure am popular," Fargo said to Chaku, and was rewarded with a hint of a smile.

"He right. You peculiar white man."

"What's so strange about howling at the moon when you're drunk?"

"You drunk now?"

"Sober as a parson." Fargo took a few more strides before saying, "So what part of Africa are you from."

"Whites call it Katonzaland. We call something else. It green land. Have much jungle and hills with grass. I miss my land. I miss it very much."

"Is that the name of your tribe? The Katonza?"

"Yes." Chaku smacked a huge fist against his broad chest. "You know what Katonza are?"

"No," Fargo admitted.

"Katonza warriors. We strong tribe. Fight many others. It make us good fighters."

"How in hell did you end up here?" Fargo asked when the big black didn't go on.

A scowl creased Chaku's expressive face. "Arabs."

"Those gents who wear sheets on their heads and ride camels?"

Chaku grunted. "They raid for slaves. Man, woman, child, they take anyone. One night they come my village. They burn huts, shoot warriors who fight, take rest. I try fight and be hit on head. When I wake I in chains. They march us many days to ocean. Put on ship. Ship bring us to America." His features clouded. "Many die on way. Not enough food. Not enough water."

Fargo could guess the rest. "You were put up for sale and the Broxtons bought you."

"Abe Broxton. The father. He like I big. He bring me to house. He have me learn white talk. He make me wear these."

Chaku plucked at his gray jacket. "I not like but must do as—"

"Enough!" Emery had stopped again. "Not another word out of you, do you hear?" he told Chaku. "If the scout has any questions about our family he can damn well ask us and not a slave."

Fargo said, "Are you anything like your pa?"

"What? No. He likes to say as how he's as different from me as day is from night. Why do you ask?"

"Because if he is, I wouldn't work for him no matter how much he paid me."

That shut Emery up.

At the stable Fargo threw his saddle blanket and saddle on the Ovaro and slipped a bridle on and had to wait while they made the stableman saddle their horses for them. From there they rode to the Dallas House so he could get his saddlebags, bedroll and Henry rifle, and to pay his bill. It left him a dollar to his name.

The Trinity River flowed through the center of Dallas. They took a road that wound along it until the hustle and bustle were behind them. Little was said. Emery was in a funk. Thad pointed out a few houses along the way and mentioned the settlers who lived in them.

Fargo's interest perked when they passed one where a pretty young woman was hanging clothes on a line. He touched his hat brim and offered his most charming smile, and she blushed.

Two hours later they arrived at a mansion on a low hill overlooking the Trinity.

Fargo no sooner drew rein and dismounted than the front door opened and out came a white-haired man using an uncommonly thick cane. He was old but he was big and he was spry and he came down the steps with the agility of a man half his age and came straight over to the Ovaro.

"Are you Skye Fargo?" he demanded.

Fargo nodded. "Who might you be?" If he had to guess, he would say it must be Thad and Emery's grandfather.

"I'm the one who is going to bash your brains in," the old man said, and raising his cane, he swung at Fargo's head.

No other series packs this much heat!

THE TRAILSMAN

**Follow the trail of the gun-slinging heroes of
Penguin's Action Westerns at
penguin.com/actionwesterns**